CURSED BY THE LOVE WITCH

A MONSTROUS HOLIDAY SERIES
BOOK 2

CHARLOTTE SWAN

CHARLOTTE SWAN PUBLISHING LLC

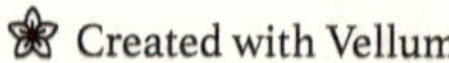 Created with Vellum

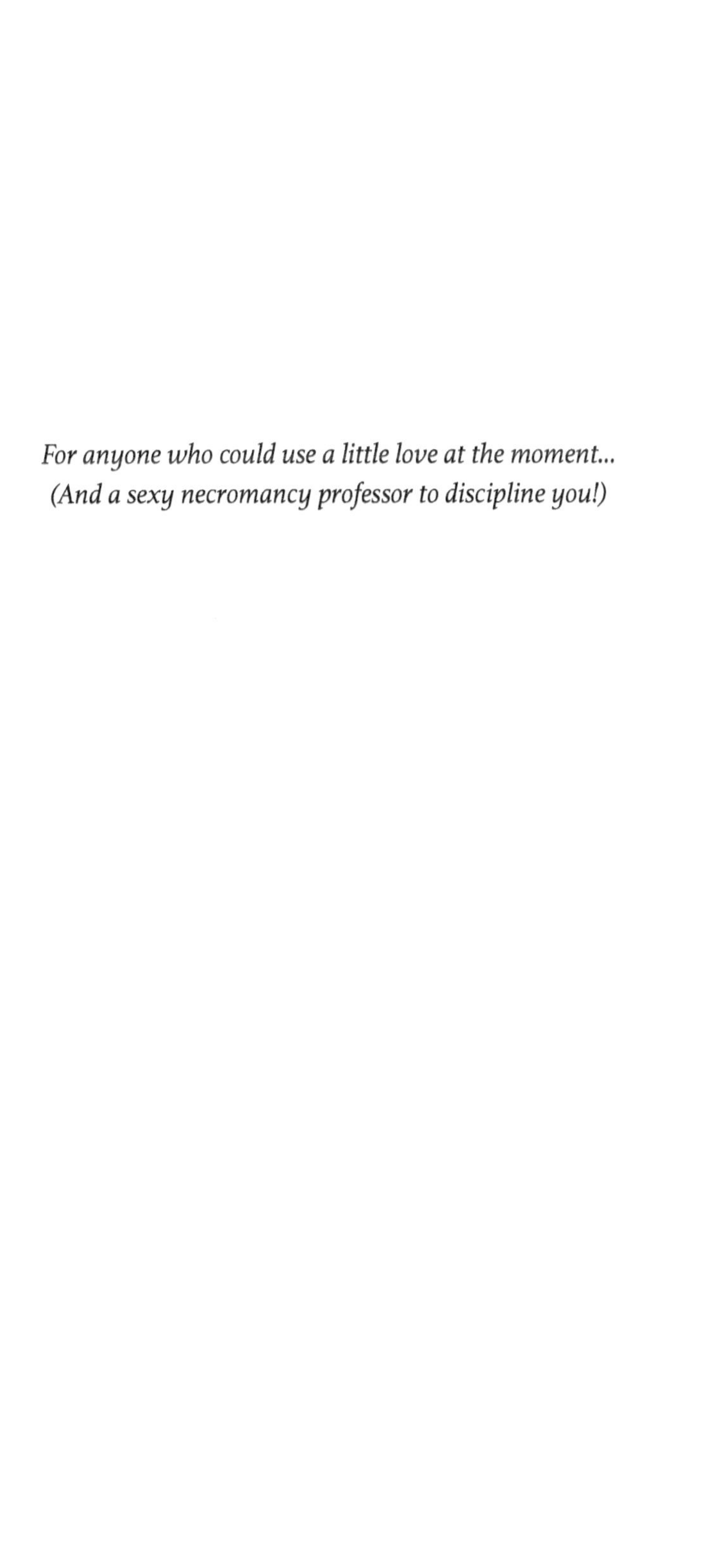

For anyone who could use a little love at the moment...
(And a sexy necromancy professor to discipline you!)

CONTENT WARNINGS

For a full list of content and trigger warnings please go to the author's website.

www.authorcharlotteswan.com

AUTHOR'S NOTE

The following author's note contains spoilers for the twist of the story.

This book is a spicy, monster romance between a love witch and her necromancy professor. Our FMC Darcee is 26 and the MMC is over 100 years old. While I try to keep their dynamic equal, please know that their relationship does begin when she is his student.

Additionally, they engage in intimate moments while she perceives him under the influence of a love potion. While we later learn that *SPOILERS* he is immune to such things I wanted you, the reader, to be aware that occurs in this book.

If you cannot read such things at this time I completely understand! For a full list of TW/CW visit my website www.authorcharlotteswan.com.

1

———

DARCEE

Lyrik and Quizton watch me closely from the other side of my wooden table.

The windows inside my dormitory are open, allowing a flower-scented spring breeze to float around the room. The fragrant air mixes with the herbal smell of an incense stick burning away atop my ceramic holder. Large pink and white candles flicker in the wind.

My large rose quartz is charging in my heart-shaped selenite bowl under the sun. A soft chime rings from my witch's bells hanging from the door. The two first years across from me are eager—studying me with wide eyes as I let my powers free and intuition wander.

I've been keeping a close eye on the two of them. Individually assessing their movements and patterns, I learned what they liked, feared, and desired above all else. Both of them had contacted me, seeking my masterful matchmaking services. As the premier—and only—love witch at Axwyne School of Magic, I take my responsibility seriously.

Hence, thoroughly examining the pair allowed me to discern that they would be a perfect match. Lyrik is a free-spirited kitchen witch with an affinity for potions, while Quizton is a logical spellcaster who can make a mean spell jar. One is a stickler for the rules, and the other is willing and wanting to bend them—a delicious combination.

Both twitch with nervous energy, stealing glances at the other. I take a deep breath, inhaling the floral scents around me and letting my power flow. Warmth slides thickly through my veins as golden light envelopes the world around me. I reach into my depths—the core of my being—and tug on the magic resting there. It is as familiar as my hand.

I watch as it casts its glow over the couple across from me. I glimpse the sparkling realm it shows me as my hands expertly flip through my *Eternal Love* tarot deck. I pause, shuffling and folding countless times, before doling out the cards in a love-spread arrangement. The two beings across from me hold their breath as I flip over the first card.

Its gold-foil face beams up at us. Lyrik lets out a delighted squeal and throws her arms around Quizton.

"I knew it," the young witch sighs. "I knew it!"

Sliding my nails underneath the card, I hold it up so it glistens in the candlelight: *the Lovers* twinkle, the female and male nude bodies embracing while surrounded by various flowers and hearts.

"The deck has spoken," I say, smiling softly. "I knew from the first moment you both came to me something was drawing you two together. Lyrik is outspoken and headstrong. While Quizton, you are quieter—thoughtful. A perfect compliment. *The Lovers* could not better indicate the affection and devotion you two share."

A look of true love passes between the pair. Such affection makes a familiar ache grip my heart, but I push it away. A love witch with no lover to call her own—I'm such a cliché.

Quizton turns to me, their dark eyes sparkling, and drops a bag of coins on my table.

"We want to do it—take the potion."

My smile deepens as I nod at the young couple.

"I thought the two of you might." With a wave of my hand, a small container with a glass topper appears. "Made this one during the last new moon. It should be extra potent."

I hand over the magenta liquid to Quizton, who clasps Lyrik's hand in their own.

"Thank you, Darcee. You're the best," Lyrik says, leading her lover towards my door.

"Oh, I know," I sigh dreamily, waving goodbye as they exit.

The smell of roses and lilacs dances in the air. I feel content—as I always do after bringing together a pair of lovers. Love is my favorite thing in the world, and while I may lack it in my personal life, bringing others together feels just as good. That's why I can't wait for graduation in three weeks.

Three weeks. That's all that separates me and the future I've dreamed of for so long. My apothecary is in the next town over—the old building is small and has seen better days. However, as I snatch up the coins Quizton left for my services and count them, a grin curves my lips. I now have more than enough for the first month's rent.

It won't be easy, but as soon as I open the doors, I'll have a long line of customers ready to find their true love.

After all, I've been bringing people together for the last five years since arriving to Axwyne. I reach for the piece of parchment atop my desk, the wax seal broken as I've already read over the letter a dozen times. Teal and Dryven were my first match I brought together. Teal came to me when I was still very new to my magic and was the receiver of my very first love reading.

My magic told me that a man would save Teal's life, and that would be the one she would call her husband. Well, as fate would have it, two days later, in potions class, a misplaced eye of newt ended up in Teal's cauldron, turning it explosive. She would've been grievously hurt had it not been for the quick thinking of Dryven, a bookish teaching assistant, who pulled her to safety just before the blast.

Teal never left his arms again, and they were married two summer solstices later. A few days ago, the letter they sent me contained a miniature portrait of the latest addition to their family, a little girl named Ever.

I hold the letter to my chest, letting the warmth thrumming through my veins intensify again. I just *love* love. As a love witch, it's kind of my thing. I always have, even when my childhood was less than ideal. In those darkest moments, I would cling to the idea of love—that one day, things would be different, and I would find my own happily ever after.

Until that happens, I'm happy to provide it to others.

The birds outside my window are singing a happy melody. My heart feels full. Thanks to my intervention, another happy couple has been brought together, making this day perfect. A shrill bell ringing cuts through my serenity. All at once, my happy mood sours, and a cold sweat breaks out across my brow.

"Oh no! I'm gonna be late!"

Hastily, I blow out the flickering candles on my desk and shuffle to find my dark cloak. I toss it on over my dress and zip myself into a pair of knee-high black boots. I fluff my curly pink hair and try to pinch some color back into my cheeks. My magenta-colored irises look tired. I'm usually drained after a love reading.

There's no time to dwell on that as I grab my books and head out the door. The dark cover of my necromancy textbook glares up at me. Why on earth did I decide to take this dreadful course?

Actually, I know why. Mistress Saege had informed me of the importance of expanding my horizons before graduation. At the same time, my best friend, Prue Starlow, told me she was enrolling in this class and didn't want to be the only non-necro-mancy student.

If only I had known Prue's motives were not because she was fascinated by the idea of reanimating corpses but so that she could make eyes at the teaching assistant, Zander, I never would've signed up. As for Mistress Saege, she believes that every obstacle is an opportunity to better ourselves.

Therefore, I am trapped into spending my final semester with the world's biggest problem—a very tall, *very* grumpy problem.

Racing down the flights of stone stairs, I make it to the main hall. I pass by countless students, all hustling off in different directions, clutching their books. A few students gather around, waving wands and making small stones float. A few girls gather over a cauldron and giggle as shapes float out from the steam—the smell of ink and smoke dance around every corner.

A few of my peers wave at me, but I can manage little more than a smile back. Finally, I reach the door to the tower and fling it open. I'm rapidly running out of breath, taking the stairs two at a time. Sweat makes my curls cling to my temples as I reach the heavy metal door and thrust it open.

I fall into the room a moment after the bell rings. Glancing around the room, I see the darkly dressed necromancy students eyeing me with familiar apprehension. I breathe deeply and note with some happiness that the High Warlock's massive desk is empty.

Fortune has smiled on me, and he surely won't notice that I was—

"Late again, Miss Thistle," a booming voice calls from the far side of the room.

My heart hammers in my chest as cold violet eyes pin me to my spot by the door. Bael Fangborne, the High Warlock of Axwyne School, looms over a bubbling cauldron. His gray skin glitters like the dark strands of his hair that curl just below his pointed ears. He is tall, the massive cauldron barely reaching above his waist. His black shirt is unwrinkled and as stiff as the male wearing it.

A lie forms on my tongue as I feel a saccharine smile shape my lips. The High Warlock merely sketches a dark brow at me.

"There is no excuse you could give for your tardiness that I would find satisfactory. You are to serve detention here tomorrow. Dawn."

I swallow down my groan. I loathe waking up early, primarily because of what's happening tonight.

"Yes, Professor Fangborne," I say, slinking towards the only open desk in the room.

Prue looks at me, an apologetic smile curving her red lips. Her dark hair is pulled back in a loose bun, and her blue eyes shimmer like crystals. I shrug and prop open my heavy textbook. Even the script inside the book is bleak. Necromancy is in such sharp contrast to my affinity. Love and Death—opposites.

Bael begins his lesson. The deep rumble of his voice skitters down my bones. It would be pleasant if I didn't abhor the male teaching us the various uses for poisons. Necromancy is such repugnant magic, especially as a pale-colored frog with its limbs stitched together appears between Prue and me at our work desk.

Zander comes by our desk to give us the ingredients for the reanimation potion. His tawny cheeks darken as his eyes linger on Prue. Color swims on her pale face as she accepts the items, and he quickly moves to the following table. I can practically see their souls coiling around each other, ready to knit together and become one.

Their show of fledgling love helps dissipate my foul mood over the thought of serving another detention with the High Warlock.

"Your love affirmations have been working," Prue whispers.

"Zander asked me to attend the Head Mistress's Spring Equinox party tonight."

"Prue!" I squeal, causing a few class members to look our way. I blush and lower my voice. "That's wonderful. I'm so happy."

"It's more than that, Darcee." She glances at Zander before looking back at me. "We've been talking and want to take a love potion."

"Are you sure, Prue?" I ask. "Is Zander sure? A love potion is no little thing."

"I'm sure," Prue says. "As for Zander—"

"I'm sure, too," a male voice says above us.

I jump in my seat at his sudden reappearance.

"Sorry." He smiles softly before turning his brown eyes on my friend. "But we are both serious about this. I want to get out of my head and embrace these feelings for Prue. We both thought a love potion could be just the thing to do it."

I nod. Love potions are no trivial thing. They can be complicated and must be administered with care. I had noticed Zander's resistance to accepting Prue, but after some digging, it was clear that some aspects of his past made him wary. A love potion can help the drinker push past those blockers and embrace their true nature. If made correctly, that is.

"Would you help us with this, Darcee? I wouldn't trust getting one made by anyone else," Prue says, touching the back of my hand.

"Without question," I sigh. "I'd be honored."

"We'd like to take it tonight, after the party—is that enough time for you to make it?"

I nod. "Plenty of time. I'll let you know when it's ready."

Zander smiles and thanks me before moving back towards the front of the class. With that matter settled and my mood vastly improved, Prue and I begin working on our potion. The ingredients are just as morose and disgusting as every other thing made in this class. Fingernails from a dead man? Where does one even purchase such a thing?

A shiver races down my spine as a chill drifts through the air. A large shadow looms above us, and violet eyes cause my hands to tremble. The High Warlock watches us closely, saying nothing. His stoic silence adds to his lack of appeal. Goddess, was there ever a male so dreadful? Maybe he unsettles me because he isn't human like the rest of us. With his pointed ears and gray skin, Mistress Saege says he's over a century old but doesn't look a day over thirty.

His eyes connect with mine, and a familiar disapproving scowl twists his face. Detention tomorrow will be awful. This isn't my first with him, but I hope it is the last. Usually, he just leaves a note and makes me sit silently in a chair while sorting through old teaching manuals before leaving. He doesn't even bother to show! Part of me believes it's a test. He watches me from where I can't see, tempting me to see if I'll go before my time is up.

I never do.

Tomorrow's will be exceedingly awful, given the equinox party tonight. Most students will celebrate and let loose, but I must ensure I don't overindulge and miss my alarm. I wonder what he'll have me sort this time. Bat corpses? Pieces of rotten flesh? I shudder just thinking about it.

The High Warlock and Zander return and watch as we feed the frog our potion. It's not as dark green as the others. The poor darling flexes its atrophied muscles, gives a meager croak, and collapses going still once more. The High Warlock says nothing, merely shakes his head before returning to his desk and announcing he has graded their previous exams.

That's another piece of this awful class. Our entire grade is made up of four exams. If you fail more than two, your chances of passing this class are nonexistent. My first exam wasn't terrible, the second was horrendous, and now the third one—

The parchment hits my desk softly, and my stomach drops as I see its grade. *Fail* is written in an elegant script. I glance up at the purple eyes searing into me.

"Mistress Saege does nothing but sing your praises, Miss Thistle. Therefore, I must assume it is only my class you decide not to apply yourself in."

He walks away on silent feet. Heat swims up my neck and inflames my cheeks. I snatch the test up and ball it in my fists. The others around me whisper, but none meet my eyes when I look up. It's as if the male enjoys embarrassing me. If he were a better teacher, he'd see that the coursework did not agree with my natural talent, and even when I apply myself, it is of very little use.

Instead of considering that, it is easier for him to deem me a slacker and that I care little for this course.

This is partially true. I have no desire to learn how to reanimate a corpse or what poisons do what, but I care deeply about this class. Namely, the fact that if I fail, I can kiss my hopes of graduation away, and the dream of opening my apothecary will remain just that.

The bell rings, and I scoop up my belongings. My eyes meet the High Warlock's one last time, and a fresh wave of annoyance rolls through me. His high cheekbones and sharp jaw remain taut as I glance away. He'd be handsome if he weren't such an awful male.

"Who? The High Warlock?" Prue asks as we make our way out the door.

I blush, not realizing I had said those thoughts aloud.

"I fear only a dreadful male could teach such dreadful material."

Prue laughs as we filter in amongst the afternoon wave of students. Most are running back to their dorms to prepare for the festivities tonight. The equinox parties are a lively affair, especially for the first years. It's typically their first real taste of magical freedom. A witch or warlock usually doesn't come fully into their power until they are twenty-one. Some are born into magical families, but for those like myself who are born to non-magical parents, coming to this school is the first time you're around others like you.

"Look on the bright side. You've had detention with him before, and he didn't even show," Prue says, nudging my shoulder.

"He was watching me, I'm sure."

I shove my hand into my pocket and feel my crumpled-up test. My feet snag on the stone floor. Prue stops next to me as bodies dodge around us. My hand begins to tremble as the weight of this test sinks into me.

"What am I going to do, Prue? If I fail this course, I won't graduate."

Prue's full lips twist.

"Have you ever considered asking the High Warlock for help?"

A humorless laugh rasps out of me.

"Like he'd do that. He loves watching me suffer."

Prue shakes her head.

"High Warlock Bael isn't all bad. Zander says he just puts on that hard-ass routine for the first years so they know what they are getting into with him. Necromancy is a serious affinity, and he has to weed out those who wouldn't treat it as such."

"Well, consider me weeded. I'd happily drop out, but the deadline has passed."

"I know he seems awful, but maybe you can ask him to help you at detention tomorrow. He is still a professor, after all."

I shrug. "Assuming he shows."

"Yes, assuming that. Now, enough worrying for today. There is fun to be had tonight!" Prue wiggles her dark eyebrows. "Are you planning to attend the equinox with someone?"

I shake my head, and my heart squeezes.

"No one's asked me."

How dreadful. It was my last equinox party, and I had no date.

A few younger warlocks pass by, cocky grins plastered on their face as they openly appraise us. A bolder one waves and winks, but none of them interest me. No one at this school has in a long time.

The air around me shifts—a dangerous chill blowing through. The hallway parts and a foreboding figure looms at the end of it. My breath catches, and for some odd reason, my heart speeds up. The High Warlock looks out of place in the sea of students. His purple eyes connect with mine, and his gaze is too intense, leaving me breathless.

"Going to Mistress Saege's," I murmur to Prue. "I'll send a raven when your potion is ready."

She tells me I'm the best, but I barely hear it. I hardly register anything around me as my gaze remains transfixed on the High Warlock. Something uncoils in my stomach, hot and demanding. It unsettles and thrills me all at the same time.

I'm the one to break eye contact first and allow the busy hall to swallow me up. I lose him in the sea of bodies and turn to walk towards Mistress Saege's room.

My heel clicks along the stone floor as I put as much distance between us as possible. Yet still, I feel his gaze searing into me every step of the way.

2

DARCEE

I get lost on the way to Mistress Saege's.

Seeing the High Warlock must've really unsettled me.

The bell rang about five minutes before I turn down the familiar hallway in the potions and charms wing of the school. Notes of fresh herbs, blooming flowers, and the distinct metallic scent of magic flow between each crack in the stone wall. Power hums—pulsing in a rhythm invisible to non-magic wielders.

A sense of righteousness flows through me. When I first arrived at Axwyne as a freshly twenty-one-year-old baby witch, this wing of the sprawling castle grounds felt the most like home. Or what I imagined a happy home would feel like. Goddess knows my home life was less than ideal.

I shove aside those unpleasant memories and allow the serenity to soothe my frazzled nerves. I need to focus. Crafting a love potion for Prue and Zander will take time, and I need to make it strong if they want it to work tonight. The potion will need time to charge to have the intended effect.

Mistress Saege's large green-painted door looms at the end of the hall. If I know Saege, she'll be busy helping the Head

Mistress with her party this evening. I've been working as her teaching assistant since my second year and have used the time in her magnificent classroom to hone my potion affinity. I pick up my pace, knowing I'll have first-year exams to grade for her on top of Prue's potion.

The hall's quiet stretches, and annoyingly, my thoughts return to Professor Fangborne. The embarrassment has faded, and now fresh annoyance spreads through my muscles and clenches my jaw. Someone ought to do something about him— I ought to do something about him, but what?

Why is he so hard on me? Shouldn't he just want to pass me along? I'm a graduating student in a first-year course. Necromancy isn't something I'm ever going to engage with again. Yet, for some reason, he has deemed it necessary for me to be proficient.

I think about what Prue suggested about reaching out to him for extra help, but his disdain for me makes me quickly dismiss that option. No matter what I'm doing, I always feel his eyes on me. The intensity of his gaze tracks my every movement. It would be alluring—flattering even—if his mouth wasn't set in a permanent scowl.

Is it because of how I dress? How I look? I'm a bit more colorful than his usual student—my pink hair notwithstanding. Does he think I'm some frivolous love witch with her head in the clouds, incapable of taking anything seriously? He claims to speak to Mistress Saege about me, and I know she would be the first to sing my praises and relay that I am one of the most dedicated students in this school.

Why do I even care what he thinks? And worst of all, why does this small, devious part of me want to impress him and earn his praise?

I let out a growl of frustration and push into Mistress Saege's room. I barely take two sets into the room when I collide with something hard. No, not something—someone.

Large hands go to my upper arms to steady me, and my head snaps up. The air freezes in my lungs.

As if my thoughts had summoned him, the High Warlock stands before me, his grip firm but gentle. He's so big; pressed this close to him, my head barely reaches the center of his chest. Those purple eyes burn with the same intensity they did in the hallway.

His hands tighten on me, and it feels pleasant. Goddess, I've been single for too long.

In an instant, he drops me as if I've burned him and steps back. I do the same, and I find myself annoyingly breathless.

"High Warlock," I say softly. I can still feel the heat of his palms through the layers of my clothes.

"Miss Thistle," he returns.

Giving me a brief nod, he passes me and exits through the door I just came in from. His long, dark cape brushes me as he passes. His smoky scent tickles my nose. It's mixed with something wild that I can't name. It travels into my lungs and overwhelms all of my other senses.

Why am I breathless? What is wrong with me? My disdain for him is now physically affecting me. Lovely.

Turning into the potion room, I inhale the heavy floral scent from the open windows. Mistress Saege always keeps it warm here. Tall wooden bookshelves line the walls laden with spell books and grimoires. Ivy crawls up along the far wall, where another towering set of shelves can be found housing all manner of spell ingredients. From dried roses to selenite to herbs from far-off lands, there isn't an ingredient you can't find here.

She'll have just what I need for Prue's potion. I had spent yesterday organizing her inventory and found she had a bottle of unused rose water—the water collected under the blood moon. Its cleansing properties will enhance my love potion nicely. I sigh contently and approach the back wall when a low sound reaches my ears.

Turning to my right, I don't know how I missed her before. Mistress Saege is slumped over her large mahogany desk. Her hands are cradling her head. Long, graying tendrils fall between her fingers. Quiet sobs shake her body.

"Mistress," I call softly, walking towards her.

She jolts in her chair, looking up at me with surprise.

"Oh Darcee, my dear, I'm oh—I'm such a mess. I didn't want you to see me like this."

She rubs at her red-rimmed green eyes and sniffs loudly. A forced smile curves her lips.

"What's wrong?" I ask, coming to stand beside her at the desk.

Her watery smile shatters as a fresh sob catches in her throat. Shaking her head, tears stream down her wrinkled cheeks and disappear into the collar of her white shirt.

"He...Bael...he—oh, I don't even know what to say. It's all too much—"

My beloved teacher—the one who's shown me nothing but kindness since I came to this school five years ago—breaks off into a fresh torrent of sobs. She rises on wobbly knees and hurries towards the spiral staircase that leads to her office above the classroom. Her cries echo around the room until she slams the door firmly behind herself.

Only then do they become heartbreakingly muffled.

Anger, boiling and all-consuming, races through my veins as I watch her leave. Bael, the High Warlock, that wretched male—now he's reduced Mistress Saege to tears. It would seem he has very little care for any of us. I am not unique. His ill treatment extends to his peers as well.

This cannot stand. Someone must do something about him, and that person must be me. I'd never wish ill on another being, but he cannot live amongst us unchecked any longer.

My mind gets to work, mulling over different ideas. Poison is too extreme, as is grievous bodily harm. There is also the matter of my skill level. I can make a mean love potion, but other than that—

That's when it hit me—a wonderfully evil idea. I cannot do it even as I consider it, but it seems like the only way. Besides, would it be so bad if the High Warlock fell asleep for a few... years?

Let's say ten or so?

That would surely end our classes and clear up the pesky issue of my grade. With no teacher available, they would have no choice but to pass us all until the course could be retaken. Not to mention, who doesn't love a long nap? The High Warlock is seemingly immortal. What's a decade to him? By then, I'd be long gone from here, and if the plot were ever found, there would be no way for them to trace it back to me.

It's ridiculous even to consider, not to mention a sleeping potion is tricky work. Yet, after years of nightmares, I've mastered the perfect formula. If I am found out, the consequences would be severe—I'd be expelled at the very least.

Saege's tearful cries reach my ears and strengthen my resolve. The High Warlock is an unkind male, and I will not let him steal away my dreams because he wishes to make his morose nature all of our problems. I'm doing this for the good of everyone. At least, that's what I tell myself.

"But love first," I say aloud.

Dropping my stuff on the nearest work table, I quickly gather the ingredients necessary. Fresh roses, rose water, pink quartz, salt for protection, cinnamon to make their love spicy—it's not long until their glittering love potion is boiling away in my cauldron. The smell is lovely and warms my heart. Reaching into myself, I picture the golden warmth flowing through me and infuse all my love and desire into their potion, increasing its potency with my love magic. This potion will be strong enough to break down any barrier between them and allow love to flow freely.

Once done, I find a small glass container to store it in. I meant to order more heart-shaped ones, but I'll have to make do with just a standard bottle. The magenta color glows brightly and is iridescent in the afternoon sun. Nestling an array of rose quartz beneath it, I rest it in the selenite charging bowl and allow its power to intensify.

Turning back to my cauldron, I pause for a moment. Is this something I want to do? Closing my eyes, I reflect on every disappointed and disdainful gaze. I feel the embarrassment he's caused me and recall Saege's tear-stained cheeks. Without another hesitation, I get to work crafting the sleeping potion. I've made so many of these that I know just what ingredients to adjust to make them long-lasting.

The transparent liquid bubbles inside my cauldron, and the minty scent stings my nose. Needing it to work quickly, I pluck a piece of my hair and drop it into the potion, stirring it with my intention. I infuse the last dregs of my magic into the liquid. Pouring it into a separate glass container, I realize with a start that it looks remarkably similar to the love potion.

It's best not to get these two mixed up.

Finding a piece of parchment, I scroll a note to Prue and attach it to the love potion. Nestling both inside the charging bowl so they can be at their strongest before tonight's festivities, I survey my handiwork. I'll bring another happy couple together tonight and eliminate the thorn in my side for the past semester.

Perhaps I am being too harsh—or I'm not as kind-hearted as many would believe—but I care little. I know what it's like to suffer under someone who goes unchecked for their cruelty. If only someone had acted bold enough when I was younger, I wouldn't have a permanent reminder of those dark times.

This is a lesson he needs to learn.

A strong breeze blows the windows open in Mistress Saege's room. The day's final bell has rung, and she has still not left her office. Inhaling deeply, I let the spring breeze calm me. Walking towards the nearest window, I push it open further and whistle for a raven. Scribbling down a quick note to Prue to collect her potion in the next few hours.

I watch the midnight-colored bird take flight.

Below in the courtyard, I can see students already making their way near the forest's edge to help begin decorating for the party. I need to start getting ready myself. Collecting my things from the workbench, I cast one last glance at my charging potions. The easy part is done.

Now, all that's left to figure out is how to get the High Warlock to ingest the potion without him noticing.

3

DARCEE

Staring at myself in the full-length mirror, I'm the picture of pink perfection.

The top half of my hair is pulled back from my face and secured with a pale pink bow that matches the color of my dress. The skirt hits about mid-thigh and flares out in a perfect complement to my lacy bell sleeves. My silver pentagram hangs from my neck and falls between my breasts, which are just slightly highlighted by the v-shaped neckline of my dress. Lastly, I slip on a pair of towering platform heels.

My magenta eyes glow, surrounded by thick, dark lashes. I've painted my lips a rich rose color to highlight the glow of my cheeks. I love these parties—I love dressing up and mingling with other students. It's typically the best place for me to find a pair of lovers who need my guiding hand to bring them together.

However, tonight is different.

Tonight is not for my enjoyment; I am a woman on a mission. While getting ready, I searched my brain for how to slip the sleeping potion to the High Warlock. A sinking feeling floods my stomach as I consider that he may not even attend the party. If so, what will I do then? I cannot think of such a thing.

This plan is rash—foolish—and yet it must be done. No actual harm will come to the High Warlock, and all of us suffering in his presence will be freed. I should be heralded a hero, but I'll take a passing grade and walking across the stage at graduation as all the thanks I need.

A sharp ringing cuts through my thoughts as the bell tolls nine times. If the High Warlock is attending the party, he won't be staying for very long. I'm running behind, and I cannot afford to wait another moment.

Securing a thick leather band around my waist, I slip out of my dorm room and hustle down the hall. Taking the winding staircases and cutting down several hallways, I finally find myself in Mistress Saege's castle wing. I push into her classroom, the stillness broken up by the intense breeze blowing in from the window. It carries voices from the party below. The wind upends several bowls of dried flowers and scatters pieces of parchment. With a wave of my hand, the window loudly clicks shut.

Walking over to the charging bowl, only one potion remains. While I was getting ready, Prue sent me a raven, telling me she had picked up her love potion. Her thanks and love had poured through the note, and I couldn't be more excited for my friend.

Oh, how *lovely* love is!

As much as I wish I could sit in this content feeling, the potion still lingering in the bowl sends a shiver down my spine. I reach for it, and my hand pauses. Again, is this the right thing to do? My intuition, which has seen me through even the darkest moments, is annoyingly silent.

The darkness of my past yawns open. Memories I've longed to suppress move my hand of its own accord, snatching up the potion and doing the one thing I didn't have the power to do before.

Act.

It will be brilliant if my poorly thought-out plan goes off without a hitch. After I slip the potion into the High Warlock's drink tonight, he'll feel ill due to the high dose. Everyone knows he lives deep within the *Wicked Woods*. His cottage is impenetrable to enter unless guided by him. He'll slumber away in there without anyone coming to look.

I'll graduate, and no one will be the wiser until he wakes. It is a selfish plan, but as I remember my humiliation and Mistress Saege's tears, my resolve strengthens further. If putting a cruel male to sleep makes me a bad person, so be it. I will not allow his disdain to rob me of the one thing I've wanted since I first discovered my magic.

With steady hands, I lift the potion. The magic hums behind the glass and tickles my palm. I uncork it and sniff—the floral scent is pleasant. The potion has significantly dulled in color. The bright magenta it once was is turning milky and pale. It must be strong to incapacitate a strong warlock such as him.

Looking inward, I find the final tendrils of my magic, which is waning due to how much spellwork I've done today. Leaving the vial uncorked, I slice the tip of my finger with my nail and watch a thick ruby droplet of my blood pool there. Blood magic is intense—necessary in only the most dire circumstances.

Most students are forbidden from using it, but Mistress Saege has been teaching me how to enhance my potions with it for years. Swallowing, I hang my finger over the lips of the container and watch the drop of my blood hit the potion. Taking a deep breath, I close my eyes and allow my warm magic to flow from me along with my intention.

"Dear Goddess, hear my plea. Strengthen this potion for me. Dear Goddess, hear my plea. Strengthen this potion for me."

I repeat the phrases over and over until the vial in my hand begins to heat. Blinking open, I marvel at the spell's rich red color. It glitters and swirls within the bottle, its power palpable. A sense of relief washes over me. This potion has received the strength of the Goddess, indicating that She approves of what I'm doing.

At least, that's what I tell myself as I secure the potion to the belt around my waist. It dangles off my hip and looks like a standard potion a love witch would have. No one will think twice when they see it, assuming it is another of my love spells I'm delivering during the party.

Slipping from the room, I make my way towards the court-yard. The voices around me rise, and I take in the revelry. Streamers of all colors blow in the breeze. Pyres have been built high and are burning fiercely. Offerings are laid out for our Gods and Goddesses to celebrate spring and the plenty it will bring. Magic flows through the air, its metallic scent cutting through the smell of fresh grass and smoke.

Several students passed me, clearly drunk. Their cheeks are ruddy, and their steps are staggering as they trot around the front lawn—a few clasps glittering sparklers in their hands as they flit between the massive bonfires. Long wooden tables are laden with food and wine for celebrating. I'm stopped briefly by Ulya, who begs me for another love reading.

I sigh softly, touching her shoulder. She is a first-year with curling brown hair and freckled cheeks. Her massive knit sweater swallows up her lush figure, and the way she curls in on herself still after all her sessions with me breaks my heart.

"As I've repeatedly said, you must listen to the cards. Weekly readings won't change anything." I narrow my eyes at her. "Now, have you been doing your self-love affirmations? Remember, no one will—"

"Love us if we don't love ourselves first. I know, and you're right. I just feel silly," she admits sheepishly. I tip up her chin and find her cheeks darkening with color.

"Everyone feels silly—especially where love is concerned. But we cannot fully accept or return another's love until we are content with ourselves."

Ulya shrugs, looking away. Something sparkles under her collar. I tuck my finger under the neckline of her wool sweater.

"What do you have on under here?" I say, spying glittery satin.

"I—well—I know you said I should start dressing for myself, so I bought this dress. My mother would never let me wear such a thing, but I liked it. I wanted to wear it tonight but thought it was—"

"Take off the sweater, Ulya. Let yourself be seen."

The young witch takes a deep breath before pulling her sweater's heavy, dark green fabric over her head. Backing up a step, I take her in. The dress shimmers in the moonlight. Silver and gold weave amongst the amethyst-colored fabric. The dress hugs her figure, showing off the fullness of her breasts and the curve of her ample hips. Dark tights give way to tall black boots, accentuating her legs. She tucks a curly strand of hair behind her ear.

"Well," she says, her eyes transfixed on the grass below her.

I smile, pulling a pin from my hair and securing the left side of her hair away from her face. She looks up at me, her green eyes glowing atop her tan cheeks.

"You look beautiful, Ulya. Don't hide anymore."

Her cheeks go up in a flash of pink.

"Thanks, Darcee. I—"

"Ulya?" a soft voice calls.

Both of us turn to see Talia, a second-year green witch. Her dark brown skin is covered in a light dusting of gold glitter that matches the golden thread woven between her braids. Her dark eyes sparkle, complimented by her olive green dress. Fresh flowers and a smattering of dried herbs containers are tucked into her belt.

She's come to me before, looking for any guidance on where her future partner could be. As I watch the two witches stare at each other, my intuition wakes from its slumber with a smile.

"Wow, you look—I've never seen you dress like this."

"I—um—well—I—"

"Ulya told me she hasn't seen the new installments in the botanical gardens. Talia, you had a hand in those, didn't you?"

Ulya gives me a wide-eyed look, but I keep a calm smile on my face. Talia glows with happiness, clearly a lover of plants.

"Oh yes, I'd be happy to show you. It is some of my best work if I say so myself."

Ulya merely blinks at her. The silence stretches long enough that I nudge her with my shoulder.

"I—yes—I'd love to see you. *It*! I'd love to see *it* with you."

Talia chuckles, linking her arm through Ulya's. At that moment, I swear I can see their souls connecting, and the look on Ulya's face is that of someone in love. The two of them turn away, absorbed enough in each other that I'm instantly forgotten, but I don't mind. Love is a wonderful thing—the best thing in the world.

Speaking of love, I notice with a smile that Prue and Zander are missing from the party—no doubt fully embracing their passion with the aid of my love potion. I'm hoping it does the trick for them.

Most people don't understand what a love potion is primarily used for. Its true purpose, which I use with my clients, is to encourage strong emotions to manifest into an overwhelming desire. Love potions are not typically used to make an unsuspecting drinker fall in love with the one who made it. Indeed, a love potion can give the illusion of affection if administered incorrectly or infused with a piece of someone's person. If the maker's blood, hair, or saliva were to find its way into the potion, it would become tainted and make the drinker fall in love with whoever's body part was inside.

That is why it is paramount that people seek out a trained love witch like myself to ensure that no contamination has occurred. Unrequited love potions are strictly forbidden; anyone caught making one will face intense punishment.

Glancing around, my eyes meet a few pairs of third-years who appraise me with lavish grins from head to toe. I can't help but laugh. My future love doesn't exist at Axwyne. I'm pretty confident of it and have given up finding him here. Who would know better than me, after all?

Still, I return their waves and smiles as I cross the grass. I shouldn't be surprised; I've always been drawn to an older man. Someone established, powerful. Someone who can—

The breath stills in my lungs as my eyes connect with a familiar violet pair. My heart pounds as I take in the High Warlock, somehow looking miserable amongst so much excitement. His dark hair is glossy in the moonlight, and his gray skin is luminous against the black cape he wears.

I try not to let his gaze unsettle me, but the rate with which I find his eyes on me is growing alarmingly frequent.

He's located on the outskirts of the crowd, with Mistress Romina Braybooke talking quite animatedly at him. The High Warlock hardly seems to notice, but at least he's dropped his gaze from me. I take in the older witch. Her hair is slicked back in a severe bun, and her lips are painted a dark red. They'd make a good couple with their shared morose nature. I once had the displeasure of finding myself in her hexes course for a semester, and I passed by the skin of my teeth.

Mistress Romina shared the High Warlock's affinity for singling me out and calling me everything but a dimwitted girl.

The older witch leans closer to his side, and I barely suppress my laugh as the High Warlock steps back. Romina barely looks ruffled as she presses on with whatever tale she's recounting. My eyes fall to the barely touched glass of sparkling red wine in the warlock's grasp. His sizable gray hand practically engulfs the whole thing.

The deep color of his wine will nicely camouflage the sleeping potion, and its pungent taste should also be well hidden by it. Now, all that's left is to figure out how to slip it into his glass without him or Romina noticing.

Glancing around the students near me, my eyes land on a familiar blonde head.

I unhook the potion from my waist, uncork it, and hold it snuggly in my palm. I only get one shot at this. Using my other hand, I wave toward Marius, who walks over to me with his familiar swagger. His golden eyes are simmering with desire, clearly aided by the full goblet of sparkling wine in his palm.

His pretty face was the first thing I noticed about him when I arrived at Axwyne. We had a fling for a few months as first-years that eventually fizzled off when I realized Marius would never be able to give me the love I truly desired. We've had a few trysts here and there over the years, but not for a long time, despite how many ravens he sends me in the early morning hours.

The scent of lavender and chamomile hit me as he saunters over.

"Darcee," he purrs.

"Marius," I return with a devious smile. "I need your help with something."

"Really?" he asks.

"But you can't tell anyone." I flutter my lashes and bite my lip.

His smile deepens, and I'm pleased my rudimentary flirting is paying off so well.

"If you wanted to start hooking up again, all you had to do was ask. I've been waiting for you to reconsider."

"Really?" I sigh, hooking my arm through his. "I'm sorry to say that isn't what I had in mind."

Marius's golden brows lower as I lead him from the crowd towards where the High Warlock looms. Luckily, it seems he and Romina have drifted a bit closer, which will make what I'm about to do more plausible.

"What have you been up to, Pink?"

"Ugh, I hate that nickname." I wrinkle my nose. "But the usual, if you must know. This and that. Decadence and depravity."

"You were always a wild one. No man has yet to tame you."

It isn't a question, but I treat it like one. We're almost there, and I need to keep him distracted.

"Why would I want a keeper?"

"As I recall, you always preferred a more dominating partner."

"Only in certain situations."

Marius laughs as we continue to walk. We are almost to them, and I feel the High Warlock's gaze upon me like a physical touch. Nerves threaten, but I cannot lose my edge now. This is my only chance, and I have to make it count. Sweat pools along my neck, but I stay focused.

When we are an arm's length away, Marius leans to whisper in my ear.

"You know I always regretted—"

I don't hear the rest of whatever flirtatious come-on he was about to deliver as I dig my heel into the lawn and take what I hope is a believable tumble directly into the High Warlock. His hard body jostles against mine as he lets out a surprised grunt. My hand goes to the top of his goblet, dumping the vial's contents into it as he helps me.

I slip my hand away, concealing the glass vial again, as a true blush breaks out along my cheeks.

"High Warlock," I say breathlessly, staring up at him.

His eyes swim with intensity, but neither he nor Romina, who I can see from the corner of my eye is glaring at me, seem to have noticed what I slipped in his drink. They were much too distracted by my fall, which was my hope. The High Warlock's hands are on my upper arms, squeezing like he had earlier in Mistress Saege's class. Through the thin sleeves of my dress, it feels as though he's touching my naked skin.

"I'm so, so sorry," I began to babble. "Here, let me—did I spill on you? I—"

"It is alright, Miss Thistle," he says in a low voice. "Are you injured?"

My mouth goes dry, and I notice his eyes take on a softer edge. Very peculiar.

"N—no."

"Take care, girl. Those shoes are ridiculous for a school function," Mistress Romina snarls, disgust dripping from each word.

Before I can respond, I watch the High Warlock's eyes harden as he turns that steely stare on the other witch.

"It is hardly Miss Thistle's fault the grass is overgrown."

Both Romina and I stare at him in shock. Of all the things I expected him to do, taking my side against the older witch was not one of them. I notice with a start that his hands are still resting against me. It feels nice—that is, it would feel nice being touched this way by someone—anyone—not just the High Warlock.

"Darcee," Marius calls, walking over to me. His arm slinks around my waist. "Are you alright?"

The High Warlock instantly drops his hands from my body and stalks back. He regards Marius with the same thin-veiled disdain I'm used to being at the receiving end of. I will admit his violet eyes have a more volatile edge as they stare at my companion, but I think little of it.

"Fine," I chirp, leaning into his side. "I apologize again, High Warlock. See you at dawn."

The High Warlock barely nods as I slip away, my plan in motion. All that's left is for him to drink it, and all my problems will be solved. Relief floods me as I allow Marius to lead me closer to the wooded area at the edge of the school grounds.

"What was all that about? The way the High Warlock looks at you—"

"He's never been my biggest fan," I say.

Marius seems to want to say more, but his eyes snag on the dark trees. He glances around, seeing just how secluded we are. A fresh grin curves his full lips. His arms wind their way around my back, tangling in the ends of my hair.

"Now that we are alone, what do you say to a quick romp in the woods? Our secret?"

I let out a hearty laugh and push up on my toes. My lips connect with his soft cheek.

"Oh, Marius, your cock isn't big enough to tempt me into accepting that offer."

Disentangling myself from him, I enter the woods and leave him blinking after me. Knowing Marius, he'll take my rejection on the chin and find a more willing partner for the evening. His true love isn't at Axwyne either, and he'll need to change a lot about himself before he finds her. I do not doubt that he will, for the right girl.

My heels click along the familiar stone path. The scent of incense and smoke leads me deeper into the woods until I reach the first clearing. Atop a large fire sits a boiling cauldron with an array of dried flowers and herbs next to it. Behind it, with her long pale arms stretched towards the moon, is Mistress Saege.

Her graying hair is braided behind her back, and her white shawl floats around her body. She is a beacon I find myself moving towards. Her mouth moves in a silent incantation. I shouldn't be intruding, but I can't help myself. The older witch's power flows from her and skims over my skin. The serenity here tickles something in my mind, and I feel the intense urge to run back and smack the High Warlock's goblet from his hand.

I shake myself from the thought and watch Mistress Saege's eyes blink open. I'm happy to see them free of tears. A soft smile pulls at her lips as she waves me forward.

"My dear, come. Let us give our offerings to the moon."

I smile and do as she bids me. We work together in quiet contemplation. I light tall taper candles and slice fresh apples to be added to the boiling cauldron. We pour bottles of fresh wine into the steaming pot, reflecting on our intentions. I open myself up for guidance and toss in a few bay leaves for good luck.

Once we are done, Mistress Saege pours me a glass of wine, and we settle atop a silk sheet on the ground. The night breeze tugs at my hair, and the moon casts us in a blue glow. Saege smiles at me over the lip of her glass goblet. Peace radiates from her and smooths over my frayed nerves.

"Are you feeling better, Mistress?"

The older witch smiles, setting her goblet down.

"Oh yes. The equinox always makes me emotional."

"I'm here if you wish to talk. Always."

"I appreciate that, my dear." Saege takes a deep, cleansing sigh. "It was nothing truly."

I nod, understanding exactly what she means.

"The High Warlock can be a cruel male," I say.

Mistress Saege's brows lower and inclines her head.

"Darcee, I hope I didn't give you the wrong impression. That somehow Bael was responsible for my tears because he upset me."

Ice encases my veins, and dull ringing echoes in my ears. I don't want to ask, but I must.

"What do you mean?"

Saege shakes her head, a few pieces of gray hair coming loose.

"The High Warlock is an intense male, to be sure. It is the nature of his kind. The things he sees and senses—it is a grave weight for anyone to bear. This is why he is so harsh with his students. Necromancy is no easy affinity. Every time you reach into the beyond, there is a chance you could be lost. Death is never something to trifle with unless you are absolutely prepared."

I sip my wine before setting it down and wiping my sweaty palms along my dress.

"If he didn't upset you, why were you crying?"

A soft smile transforms Saege's face.

"Have I ever told you about Symon? My twin brother. He and I were inseparable, the way all twins are. Our powers manifested around the same time, and his dream was to attend Axwyne and become a potions master." Tears pool at the edges of her green eyes. "He fell ill the summer before we were set to enroll here. Nothing could improve his condition, and he passed the day before classes began."

"Oh, Mistress," I say, taking her small hand in mine. "I'm so sorry for your loss."

"Thank you," she says, wiping her eyes. "He would've made a fine warlock—an even finer professor. As you know, it is the equinox, the veil between the living and the dead thins. Bael came to tell me that my brother had reached out to him. He wanted me to know how proud he was of me and the witch I had become. That he is waiting for me on the other side where we will be reunited again."

The world around me tilts, and I feel bile race up my throat. I drop Saege's hand and jump to my feet. My mind races, and I feel unsteady. Oh Goddess, what have I done?

Saege rises before me.

"I apologize if I gave you concern. My tears were very much of the happy variety. I would've shared it with you, but I was sending a raven to my mother to tell her what Bael shared with me."

I nod, no longer feeling attached to my body.

"I—I'm sorry. I have to go."

Turning on shaking legs, I walk quickly back up the path. Saege calls after me, but I keep moving. Bael's treatment of me is one thing, but for the kindness he's shown my favorite teacher, he doesn't deserve a ten-year slumber. I should've waited to collect more information, but I was ready to believe he was evil. My prejudice made it easier to think that he was irredeemable, and it was easier for me to go forth with my plan.

His treatment of me is wrong, but what I have done is just as bad. How could I have been so foolish? I've risked everything by giving him that potion. More than that, I'm stealing years of someone's life. I'll never forgive myself if I don't stop this.

I break through the woods and see that the party has begun to dissipate. A few students and professors still linger, but it's clear most have returned to the dorms for the evening. My eyes scan the courtyard. My hands shake as minutes tick by, and I can't see the formidable form of the High Warlock.

My eyes snag on Romina's dark head, and I approach her. She turns towards me like a viper ready to strike. Her pretty face is twisted in anger.

"Where is the High Warlock?"

Romina's dark eyes narrow.

"What concern is that of yours?"

I don't let her sharp tongue deter me.

"I meant to ask him about the spellwork he assigned if he hasn't retired for the evening." The lie easily rolls off my tongue.

Romina huffs a humorless laugh.

"Unfortunately for you, your run-in with him early left him

in a particularly foul mood. He went back to his cottage half an hour ago."

Dread curdles my stomach, and my knees threaten to buckle.

"Was he feeling well?" I whisper.

"What?" she snaps.

"How was he feeling when he left? Ill at all?"

"The High Warlock didn't discuss his mood with me. Despite my best efforts."

The older witch turns from me on her dark heel. The fires around me flicker, and the flames lick along my skin. I wait for the goddess to strike me down—to lose my powers for misusing them.

"What have I done?" I whisper up towards the moon.

It doesn't answer. For the first time since I arrived at Axwyne, I feel entirely alone.

4

———

THE HIGH WARLOCK

Unease races through his veins as he lays in bed tonight.

He is unsettled like he has never been before. The familiar room feels stifling. He's sweating even though he is only dressed in silk sleeping pants. The windows are open, letting in the earthy scent of the woods around him. A breeze blows over his heated skin, causing him to thrash.

The High Warlock is being eaten alive—consumed by thoughts of her again.

No, *no*, he won't give in. He has been strong thus far and will continue to be so. But why? Why has he allowed himself to continue to suffer like this? And why, of all nights, is this one where the primal parts of himself he's kept contained for over a century are finally rising to the surface?

It's because of her, of course. Seeing her with that boy and their apparent familiarity had annoyed him. However, it is because that boy was not watching her carefully enough that the High Warlock was blessed with the feel of her.

Soft and warm and so very pink. He longs to trace her blushing cheeks with his tongue.

The idea claws at him, causing him to thrash further. A fresh torrent of emotions races through him, and the silk sheets around him tangle. He longs for the release he's never felt. The release he believed he'd die before ever experiencing.

But now he lays in bed, unsure. Thinking dangerous thoughts and wondering, not for the first time, if he was wrong to resist her. There is still a chance—a small one. Does he not owe it to himself to try? What's the worst that could happen if he does?

He needs to stop being a coward. He knows he'll always regret it if he doesn't act now.

A fresh wave of heat rolls through him as he turns over. Sleep beckons, and he knows it won't be dreamless. It will be filled with the same images of pink hair and rosy cheeks that always seem present.

He knows that when dawn breaks, nothing will be the same.

5

DARCEE

Soft tweeting followed by rhythmic taps at my window wakes me.

With a groan, I blink my eyes open, only to be greeted by darkness. How long have I been asleep? A few hours, maybe. When I returned to my room last night, I couldn't get my head to stop spinning. There was still a chance he hadn't taken the potion—it was the last bit of hope I was clinging to.

I considered taking my sleeping dram but worried I wouldn't wake up for detention. If you had told me yesterday that I was eagerly awaiting the High Warlock's arrival at dawn, I never would've believed you. Yet, as I rise from my mused sheets and strip out of my dress from yesterday, I'm praying to the Goddess that he's there.

The burnt remnants of my good luck spells still lay in ash on my desk. I poured everything into undoing my mistake until exhaustion forced me into bed. I dress solemnly for the occasion, donning a white collar shirt and black skirt before tying my cloak around my neck.

Scraping my hair back into a high ponytail, I grab my books

and exit my room. Hardly anyone is stirring this early, especially after last night's party. Most are indeed already nursing a rough hangover. I wish a sore head was the only thing plaguing me this morning.

The scent of fresh grass and misty morning air filter in through the open windows. My heeled boots clack along the stone floor. The eerie silence leaves me with nothing else to do but think.

After learning about what he did for Mistress Saege, I see the High Warlock in a different light. While he may have disdain for me, I can understand it to an extent. The subject he teaches is dangerous, and my lack of understanding is cause for concern. Buried beneath the disapproval, is there a part of him worrying about my safety?

I may be cutting him too much slack in that case. Still, I can admit what I did was rash and ill-advised. My temper was flaring hot yesterday, and I made an angry judgment call. If I want to be a good witch, I cannot allow my emotions to override my common sense like that.

I thought this final year would be my chance to start a new chapter. After graduation, I would open my apothecary and never look back again. It would be the final cutting of a cord I've still been hanging on to. Now, I fear I've ruined whatever fresh start I could've had before it even began.

I could kick myself for being such a fool.

The journey to the tower was quick due to the lack of foot traffic. The door before me looms, the last barrier before I face what I've done. When he doesn't show, what shall I do? Raise the alarm? Continue as I would before and never own up to my actions?

Warmth licks over the side of my face as the morning sun rises—streaks of gold and pink filter in through the stained glass window. With a deep sigh, I grip the door handle and pull it. The metal groans and echoes up the stairwell after me.

Pushing into the room, I take in the stillness. No one is here, and the room is cloaked in shadow. The last tendrils of hope leave me, and I collapse against the nearest worktable. My throat closes, and tears seep from my eyes. I was close to getting everything I wanted, but now I've ruined it.

I have to confess.

I'll find Mistress Saege and tell her. My punishment will be swift. I can kiss my future apothecary goodbye and any hopes of bringing more lovers together. A fresh sob falls from my lips, and I almost collapse to the floor.

Why hadn't I tried another path? Why did I even think—

The door behind me creaks open, and I nearly jump out of my skin. I whirl around, my eyes falling on the male who's just walked in. His eyes—violet eyes I never thought I'd see again—are bloodshot with dark shadows under them. He's dressed in black satin pants and a matching shirt. His cape drags behind him like spilled ink.

"You're here," he whispers.

I nearly sag with relief at the sound of his deep voice. He didn't take it. Merciful Goddess. She heard my prayers and took pity on me. The High Warlock takes a tentative step forward. His eyes are wild, as if he were seeing me for the first time. He's probably thrown off by how happy I am to see him.

"Detention," I say, my voice cracking on the last word.

His eyes widen as he stares at me intently. The High Warlock traces along the tears drying on my cheeks. I try to stand even though my knees still feel weak.

"You were crying. Why?" he asks sharply.

I shake my head, a laugh bubbling out of me.

"They're tears of joy."

The side of his mouth kicks up, and I'm happy that the desk supports me. A smile from the High Warlock is shocking enough to send me staggering to the floor.

"Joy, is what you feel spending a morning's detention with me?"

I nod. "Believe me, there's nowhere else I'd rather be."

His eyes flash, and he sucks in a breath. Slowly, he approaches, his earthy scent tickling my nose. I lean back against the desk. My head tilts up to keep his gaze. His eyes dip down to my lips momentarily, and I watch his hands fall to either side of me.

"I feel the same," he whispers.

Our bodies are so close, and I'm nothing if not confused. This is unexpected. I'm feeling a little off-kilter because I expected to find him in a sleep meant to last a decade. Therefore, my brain is slow to catch up to the fact that the High Warlock is very close.

And is looking at me like he wants to devour me whole.

His face looms close to mine. My eyelashes flutter at the heat I can feel pouring from his body. I'm shocked by how pleasant I find it. I'm now drifting closer towards this male that I've spent weeks loathing. Yesterday, I wanted him out of my life forever. Now, my face is tilting up towards his.

His nostrils flare, and his eyes blaze deeper.

"High Warlock," I breathe. "What are you—"

"Call me, Bael," he whispers. "Please."

"I don't—"

"Don't make me beg. I will."

My mouth goes dry at his words. What is happening? I've never seen him like this. He's typically so aloof and cold. Being near him had always put me on edge, and now I watch his hands slide closer to me on the desk. When they reach me, what will he do? Our bodies are so close that my chest will brush him if I breathe too deeply.

Licking his lips, his voice drips like warm honey all over my skin.

"Please, little witch. Say my name. I need to hear it from your perfect mouth."

"I—" Speechlessness is not something I've ever been afflicted with.

However, as his hands go to the curve of my waist and mine rise to his strong shoulders, I find nothing to say. I'm on fire. His touch is burning me alive. He may as well be feeling my naked skin. Part of me wants to rub all over him like a kitten—purring and preening for his attention.

It's like we are two puppets, and the universe is pulling our strings. If I were an objective third party, like I usually am in these situations, I could see how something like this could happen. After spending weeks together, we would find unbridled passion buried beneath the disdain and annoyance.

Hate and love are two sides of the same coin.

His hands grip me tighter, and I feel his warm breath against my lips. It feels nice—more than pleasant. It feels as if he stops touching me, I'll die. I've been lonely for so long. However, I can't remember ever feeling this alight by being touched by another. Even in our headiest days, Marius didn't have this sort of effect on me. It's confusing and wrong.

Wrong.

Yes, this is very wrong. He is my teacher—my teacher who is letting me fail his course, my teacher whom I feel nothing but hatred for—yes, I hate him. Don't I? Maybe hate is too strong. Regardless, we have to stop this. Now.

Beyond him being my teacher, he's decades older than me. He isn't human. Yet, that knowledge sends a delicious thrill down my spine. His lips are so close. Tempting me to meet them with my own. What would they feel like? Would they be warm? Would they part and—

His thumbs drag along my ribs, and the sensation rocks me back into my body.

"What are you doing?" I demand. My hands fall from his shoulders and give a shove to his chest.

The High Warlock—Bael—stumbles back. His chest rises and falls as if he's been running. Long, gray fingers grip the table behind him, turning white. Blinking several times, he shakes his head.

"I'm—I'm sorry, Darcee—Miss Thistle."

Licking my lips, I swallow against my dry throat, trying to forget how much I enjoyed his touch.

"It's okay," I say softly. "Things happen."

That's putting it mildly. He's just come on to me. My teacher—Bael, and I liked it. I more than liked it. There must be something wrong with me. Has my loneliness made me this desperate for any sort of attention? I slipped him a sleeping potion, and then, not even twelve hours later, I was considering kissing him.

I rub my hand against my forehead.

"No," he says, locking our gazes once more. "I'm sorry for being so awful to you all this time. I also wish to apologize for coming on strong just now—it wasn't my intention—it's just....I've made a few realizations recently."

"About what?" I ask.

"You." The breath freezes in my lungs.

"Me? I thought you hated me?"

His eyes widen.

"Hated you? No, I hold you in the highest esteem."

I let out a humorless chuckle.

"My grade and your demeanor towards me in this class state otherwise."

He cringes at my words.

"I realize now I may have been overly harsh on you. Allow me to rectify that."

I hold my breath as he walks past me and towards his desk. Reaching into the mess of drawers, he pulls a stack of papers and beckons me over. Curiosity gets the better of me, and I follow. He sets out the parchment, and I pick one up, recognizing it immediately.

"My old exams."

He nods, tucking a longer piece of dark hair behind his pointed ear.

"I wanted to offer you the opportunity to retake your old exams and improve your grade before the end of the semester."

I sketch a brow.

"I appreciate that, but if I couldn't pass them before when the lesson was fresh, I don't know what good retaking them now would do."

Bael runs a long finger over the front of one of my old tests. I observe him, noting the color dancing on his cheeks. Surely, the formidable High Warlock isn't blushing.

"I offer to reteach you the subjects one-on-one. We'd meet daily to review each lesson, and then I'd let you retake the tests."

It's the second time in the last ten minutes Bael has rendered me speechless. It can't be that easy. I was desperate to change my grade—so desperate that I concocted a sleeping potion to solve my problems. Now, I'm being allowed to fix them properly.

"That's very generous of you," I whisper.

He glances up at me, his eyes swimming with hope.

"Maybe then you would be more willing to let me prove myself."

"Prove yourself?"

"I'm not very good at this, so I'll just come out and say it." He straightens his spine and pins me with a warm stare. "I like you, Darcee. I'd be honored if you allowed me the chance to show you just how much."

My mouth falls open. Of all the things he could've said, I never expected that. Who is this male, and who replaced my hard-ass necromancy professor with him? There is an eager-ness to him—an almost boyish-like whimsy to his gaze. That stiff demeanor has melted away, and now all that's left is the male underneath it all. A male I don't think many have seen.

"I'm sorry I came on so strong before." His violet eyes darken. "Seeing you in here—it did something to me. Since last night, I realized I'm done hiding how I've felt for you. I had to tell you the truth."

"The truth—that you like me, *like me*?" I ask.

"Very much. Is that so hard to believe?"

"Yes."

"Why?"

"Why?" I repeat. "Well, for one, you've been nothing but cold and dismissive to me since I stepped foot in your class. Not to mention, it's highly inappropriate for us even to be having this conversation. You're my professor. If anyone overheard us, we'd be in trouble."

"You're more than worth the risk," he says. "But I under-stand its optics do look bad. You're graduating in a few weeks. I can be discreet until then."

He clears his throat.

"That is, um, again, all depending on you. If you feel nothing for me, my offer to help with your grade still stands. Just tell me now, and we'll never have to speak of this again. I swear to you."

I take in this confusing male before me. His eyes are clear, yet there is a feverish intensity to him. What has brought on this sudden change? It would be easier to believe he was replaced by some unknown twin than to accept that my surly necromancy professor is capable of feelings, wildly romantic feelings for me, that have seemingly manifested overnight.

It's almost like—

My stomach tips and bile crawls up my throat. I look at him, really look at him. The flushed skin, the sparkling eyes, the frenzied energy. All the signs are there. Normal people wouldn't pick up on them, but I do. It's my job to see them—and, more importantly, make them appear.

He's clearly under the effects of a love potion. But how? When could he have possibly—

I smack myself in the forehead with the palm of my hand.

Prue's silence last night no longer seems so innocent. Oh Goddess, what have I done now? I'm swearing off making potions for a good while. I'm not out of this mess just yet.

"Darcee?" Bael asks, his voice concerned.

"I—I have to go," I say.

His shoulders slump. A look of defeat haunts his eyes.

"Of course, I understand. I was foolish to think—hope— that you would be open to such an idea. My offer of tutoring remains if you wish it."

The look on his face tugs at my heart. The love potion I gave him was a powerful one. Not to mention the enhancement because of my blood. It will be in his system for a while. I'll come clean once my suspicions are confirmed and I find Prue's sleeping body. Then, I'll find a more experienced witch to make him an antidote.

If I tried to tell him the truth now, in his current state, he would just deny it. He believes himself in love with me, and I don't want to cause him any more distress. In this fragile state, he needs to be handled with care. A rejection when the potion is so freshly ingested can have harsh consequences.

With a sigh, I round to his side of the desk. My hand goes to his arm, and he looks down at me. As wrong as it is, I much prefer this male. If this is how Bael acts when he is in love, the person he is meant to be with will be in for a treat.

"Look, I just need some time to think. This is all happening very fast."

Slowly, his hand raises, pausing, waiting for me to say no. When I don't, I feel the warm press of his palm against my cheek. I suck in a breath at the gentle touch. It makes me ache in ways I never have before.

"Not for me. I've felt this way about you for as long as I can remember."

I hide my cringe as best I can. Goddess, why did I have to make the potion that intense? I lean into his touch and watch him hiss out a breath. I allow myself this moment to revel in his comfort.

"I need to check on something, but I'll see you later. For class."

He nods once before dropping my cheek.

Walking to the desk, I quickly scoop my books up and head for the door. I pause for a moment, and I will myself not to look back. It matters little as I feel his eyes upon me down the stairs and into the main hall.

6

―――――

DARCEE

Gently, I stroke Prue's soft hair as she lays atop the infirmary bed.

I hold my breath, waiting for her eyes to flutter open. Zander is resting deeply on the cot beside her. The healer said it shouldn't be long now. Mistress Nya flits around to a few other patients in her care.

Finding Prue and Zander had been surprisingly easy. The two of them had taken the potion in Prue's room, intent on spending the equinox party more intimately. However, they never got the chance, and I discovered the two draped over each other in Prue's bed.

I had spun a little tale to Mistress Nya about the two of them unknowingly taking a sleeping dram, and she drafted an antidote to give them. Then she told me there was nothing else to do but wait for them to wake up.

The silence of the infirmary stretches. I stare at Prue's sleeping form, her breathing deep and even. Shame makes my skin itch. I was so careless yesterday with Bael and my best friend. That potion could've hurt her and Zander. I should've personally delivered the love potion to them. Maybe if we had spoken before and I told her of my plan to deal with Bael, she could've talked me out of it.

I grab her hand and adjust my position on the stiff wooden chair. Already, my back is aching.

"It will be alright, dear," Mistress Nya's soothing voice says from beside me. "They'll wake up soon."

I nod, giving her a small smile.

"That antidote you made was marvelous. Have you ever made one for a love spell?"

There are subtler ways I could've approached it, but at this point, I'm desperate for this to all be over. If she can make one, I'll slip it back into Bael's drink next time we meet and be done with this whole mess.

The healer raises a brow, and I shrug.

"Antidotes were never my forte, and I'm nosey enough to wonder if any of my matches have to come to you seeking to undo what I've done for them."

Mistress Nya chuckles before shaking her head. Dark curls coil around her delicate ears.

"A sleeping potion is easy enough to undo. No matter their potency, they all contain primarily the same ingredients. Love potions are a different beast. Due to them being highly personalized, it's hard to create an antidote unless you know every element used to make it. In my experience, trying to undo one often makes the situation worse. It's best just to let those run their course. A love spell's potency dies rather quickly. As I'm sure you're well aware."

Mistress Nya's eyes narrow slightly.

"And I'm sure I don't have to tell you that any love potion administered to an unknowing recipient is something that must be reported to the Head Mistress."

I keep my smile sincere even as I feel my inside contract.

"An innocent question, I assure you. I only deal with happy couples who give me written and verbal consent."

"Good. Now quit fretting."

Mistress Nya disappears, and I take a deep breath. Great. With the option of antidoting off the table, for now, the only thing I can do is put up with Bael's *love* until the potion wears off. It shouldn't take too long with a male of his size, but I hoped all of this could be wrapped up today.

With my future apothecary flashing before my eyes, going to Mistress Saege is also off the table. My beloved teacher would be honor bound to tell the Head Mistress, who happens to be her wife. I'm out of options.

The only bright side is that Bael's true feelings for me will also quickly burn through the potion. Nya is correct when she says a love potion dies quickly. Deep down, Bael cannot stand me despite what he thinks he feels. When he realizes that as the potion's strength begins to wane, he'll hopefully be willing to allow me to fix my grade.

As awful as I am for considering it, this may be the only chance to pass his class. I shouldn't exploit his so-called feelings for me, but I shouldn't pass up on this opportunity. He won't fail the witch he believes himself infatuated with. As for his romantic advances, that's where things get a little trickier.

I didn't hate how he looked at me—far from it. I had even been thinking of kissing him at one point. I must play along a bit if I want the potion to run its course gracefully. It should be easy enough with a male who looks at me like I hung the moon just for him.

Our need to remain secretive will also help us not take things too far—even if his touch had been a surprising delight. I must keep my wits about me. When the potion fades, his memories surely will not. Hopefully, he'll be so repulsed with the idea of himself wanting me that he won't question where the feelings came from.

I'm manifesting that the embarrassment he'll feel after this ordeal will ensure his silence.

That way, I can take my passing grade, graduate, and never look back.

It is risky to dance this fine line while a love potion is in the mix, but I see no other options at the moment. Additionally, I'd never take advantage of him in this situation, my improving grade notwithstanding. That is why it is paramount that I keep our relationship flirtatious—heady—but void of any real action.

Whatever desire he feels for me now will be gone in a week or so. The rejection—which is to be expected—will still sting. I should protect myself by not getting too attached and taking things too far.

A sharp inhale pulls me from my thoughts.

Prue's bright blue eyes blink open. With a groan, she rubs the side of her head.

"Water," she croaks.

Fetching her a glass, I help her sit up, the cot squeaking beneath her.

"Small sips," I say.

She clears her throat, her eyes still looking far off.

"What happened? Zander and I took your potion and then —" Her eyes land on Zander next to her. Her sharp inhale tears at my heart, and I feel fresh tears pool in my eyes. Taking her hand, I hold on to it tightly.

"Prue, I'm so sorry. I made two potions yesterday. One was my sleeping dram, and the other was your love potion."

I hate lying to my best friend, but it is the only way. If I want to stay at Axwyne, no one can know what I did.

"I left a piece of parchment on the one you were supposed to take."

"I didn't see a note." Prue takes another small sip from her glass.

My stomach sinks further.

"I know. I found it under one of the tables in Mistress

Saege's room. It must've blown off after I left. I only realized the mistake when I collected my sleeping dram this morning."

Prue nods, setting down her glass of water.

"The potions looked so similar, I thought I knew which was the right one. We were both excited to take it, and I just guessed." Her hand tightens in mine. "I shouldn't have done that. I was careless, Darcee. I should've waited and asked you which was the correct one. Can you ever forgive me?"

A surprised rasp leaves me. I stand and settle myself on the cot beside her.

"Only if you forgive me for being such a careless witch. I ruined your night with Zander."

"Actually, I had a pretty incredible dream about him."

"Oh?" I ask, wiggling my eyebrows. "Do tell."

"Later," she says with a grin.

Her thin arms wrap around me, and we hug. I inhale her lavender scent and let it ground me. This will be over soon—a week at most, and things will return to normal.

"What happened to it?" Prue asks as we pull apart.

"To what?"

"The love potion you made for us. Once Zander and I have recovered, I thought we could try retaking it."

Waving a dismissive hand, I try to keep my voice neutral.

"It had gone off during the night. I'll make you two a fresh one. And personally deliver it this time."

Prue chuckles, settling back against the pillows.

"You're the best, Darcee." A yawn sneaks up on her. "This sleeping potion is no joke. How bad is your sleep schedule to need such a thing?"

I laugh even if it sounds brittle to my ears.

"I only take a sip each night. Not the whole bottle."

"Right," Prue says, the word fading as her eyes begin to close.

Leaning down, I press a kiss to her smooth brow.

"Sleep," I whisper. "I'll check on you later."

Prue is already asleep as I collect my things and hear the bell signaling the start of the school day. Excited voices filter in from the halls. I turn to walk out of the infirmary and leave my slumbering friend behind.

I don't know how I'm going to focus. All my thoughts are of Bael as I walk through the hall. *Three weeks*, I think. *Three weeks until graduation, and you'll never see him again.*

At least, that's what I tell myself.

7

THE HIGH WARLOCK

The hours have been tortuously long.

Each lecture had gone on and on until the seventh bell chimed. The primal part of him stirred, knowing he would get another glimpse of her. It had called him a fool for not claiming her in here when they had been alone. He had to remind himself that he wasn't a beast and that she deserved to be courted properly.

That is if she was willing to give him a chance.

The familiar faces of his introductory necromancy course file in, each seeking his validation, but he pays them little attention. He is waiting for her arrival.

A glimpse of pink hair sends blood rushing through his veins. She's on time for once and enters his classroom dressed as she was this morning, if only a bit more wrinkled. Once she is over the threshold, her eyes find him and hold—a delicate pink breaks out along her cheeks as she walks to her desk. A growl threatens to exit his throat, but he swallows it down.

His gaze on her drops as a few students come seeking advice on enrolling in his second-year course next semester. He grows irritated even as he manages to answer their questions.

As a professor, he takes his job seriously and realizes spending an entire hour staring at the pink-haired goddess that's tempted him for years is irrational.

Even if that's all he wants to do.

The final bell rings and everyone finds their seats. Darcee hangs her cloak off the back of her chair. Her thin white shirt perfectly highlights her frame. A few pink curls cling to her temples. Her partner is noticeably absent, as is his teaching assistant, Zander. He heard something about them accidentally ingesting a sleeping potion.

It matters little. This gives him an opportunity he would be a fool to pass up.

She folds her small hands atop the books on her desk. Her magic pulses under her ivory skin. He can see it—taste it. Its warmth radiates from her and into him. When her eyes meet his again, everything in him tightens painfully. He watches her sink her teeth into her full lower lip, and he nearly doubles over.

Discovering she had enrolled in his course had been a blessing and a curse. After watching her from afar all these years, being so close to her was a delight, even if it drove him mad simultaneously. In the beginning, he resented her for how she made him feel. Now, he sees how foolish that was.

She tempted the beast inside him, and he had pushed against it—fighting his very nature. Now, he would happily supplicate to her every whim if she merely said the word. It was a sudden revelation but no less true.

His gaze lingers on her a moment longer, delighting as her flush spreads lower across her chest. He remembers the feeling of her in his arms. Too quick—he was too quick, and like a little lamb, she had turned skittish. He will court her properly even if he must be discreet about it.

"Students," he says, voice clear and even. "We will continue with our reanimation potions this afternoon. Working with your partner, follow the instructions in your manuals to create the brew before administering it to your subject."

With a wave of his hand, cauldrons and supplies appear on each table. Darcee bites her lip and glances at the space beside her. He is barely able to suppress his grin. He stalks towards her slowly.

A dark-haired first-year sitting at the table beside Darcee stands.

"High Warlock, we can add Darcee to our group since her partner is absent."

Darcee gives him a soft, grateful smile. The young warlock blushes even as the High Warlock gives a dismissive shake to his head.

"That won't be necessary, Remus." He can hardly believe his voice sounds clear while his blood is a raging inferno. It heats further when he stands beside Darcee at the work table.

"I will assist Miss Thistle during today's lesson."

8

———

DARCEE

I watch in awe as Bael expertly crafts the reanimation potion.

He barely glances at the manual but talks through each step in depth with me. He shows me the difference between cutting and dicing and how you must grind everything into a fine powder to ensure all ingredients are dispersed evenly to achieve the desired result.

"Reanimation is all about balance. Even the smallest thing can throw it off and ruin the potion."

I watch him add moon water to a gray powder before turning it into a paste. He then uses that to drop dollops into the boiling cauldron.

"I never would've thought to do that," I say.

His lips twitch as if he is suppressing a grin. Working with him has been surprisingly easy. Our movements feel naturally in step with each other.

"It's simple really. Grave dust enhances the property of the nail shavings. Mixing them with moon water further strengthens them. The paste will ensure our potion doesn't become too thin and will lack the necessary potency to work." He nods to the small bowls laid out before me. "You try."

Biting my lip, I nod. Doing exactly what he did, I sift the grave dust and nail shavings into a separate bowl before slowly pouring in the moon water. It takes a few tries to get the consistency right, but I smile and look at him once it's the thickness of wet sand. His eyes glow with approval, and it sends a thrill through me.

"Excellent, Darcee."

I watch his large hand slide along the top of the work table before coming to rest atop mine. My eyes dart around the room, but everyone is too absorbed in their work to notice.

"I had a look through your old exams," he whispers. My face heats, preparing for a cutting remark about my lack of work ethic. "I realize now what the problem is. It wasn't that you weren't trying or doing the required reading—I'm ashamed to admit I believed that to be the case for a while. However, it is now clear that you've been doing all the work backward because your natural affinity contrasts necromancy. It's why you wouldn't think of making a paste with the grave dust. You're used to potions being thin and everything working in tandem. That is not the case with dark magic."

The gray skin of his cheeks darkens, and his eyes blaze.

"You have exceptional skill, Darcee. A seasoned professor like myself should've noticed that sooner and offered assistance." His hand squeezes mine. "I apologize for failing you."

My mouth feels dry. Never in my life would I have expected this—for Bael to acknowledge what I always thought was the case in this class. Prue may have been right; if I had come to him, he would've made this discovery earlier, and I would never have been in this position. Even without the love potion, I can see the male he is under the surface. His gruff nature is due to what Mistress Saege said. These potions are serious.

Necromancy is dark magic, and it takes a particular type of warlock to master it the way he has. Yet that doesn't mean he lacks total compassion. I'm a testament to that. My smile at him is genuine as I step closer and keep my voice low.

"You're going to help me now, though. Right?" I blink up at him. "If your tutoring offer still stands, I would very much like to accept it."

Biting my lip, I can't believe what I'm about to do. I don't give myself a moment to reconsider and lose my nerve.

Slipping my hand from underneath, I drag my hand along the top of his. He inhales sharply as our bodies drift closer. Looking up at him through my lashes, my smile takes on a more sensual edge.

"Among other things," I add breathily.

I have to lean into this for now. A little flirting on my part will keep the potion stable. If he senses me pulling away, it could intensify and prolong the effects, which we both cannot risk.

Additionally, once the potion is over, if he remembers me being into this, perhaps he'll be kind enough not to press the issue or seek me out again.

His eyes darken as he nods.

"Everything I offered you is still very much on the table."

"Good," I say, reaching across him to pick up a pair of tongs.

Our bodies brush, and the heat of his burns through my clothes. I stay partially bent over the table and look up at him as I pluck a mummified figure from the end of the table.

"This goes in next?" I ask.

Bael nods, his fingers curling into the desktop. Rising to my full height, I allow our hips to brush as I drop the dead finger into the boiling cauldron. Bael hisses beside me, and I can't suppress my giggle. It's awful to admit, but I'm enjoying myself.

I haven't had anyone to seduce in a long time. I should relish this while I can.

Reaching to stir the potion, I notice the tremble in his hand. Another soft giggle bubbles out of me, and his eyes dart to mine. His lips pull into a very un-Bael-like grin. If only he had been like this all the time, maybe then—

I shake myself, refusing even to consider it. This isn't real.

"What's next?" I ask softly.

"That depends," he says.

"On?"

"If I want to be a good male and finish this potion with you before assigning you all four hours of take-home spellwork."

My hand falls to my chest in mock outrage.

"Spellwork over the weekend? Don't be so cruel." I lean in closer, dropping my voice into the softest sigh. "What is the other option?"

"That I dismiss class now, bend you over this table, and see how pink you are everywhere."

A soft sigh leaves me, and I nearly fall against him. The mouth on this warlock causes me to heat in places I haven't in a long time. My hand slides slowly towards him before slipping under the fabric of his silk shirt. The fine muscles of his back play against my fingers.

You would think I was the one who ingested a love potion the way I'm acting. It's as if my body has a mind of its own. I once more feel like a puppet on the string, and the one controlling me is fueled by depraved desire.

"Those are quite the choices, High Warlock," I sigh. "Might I suggest we—"

I don't get the chance to finish as a flurry of movement catches my attention. Two students are walking towards us, and I reluctantly slide my hand and body away. Goddess, I'm losing it. I need to be more careful.

The last thing I need is for someone to discover what is

happening between us and ask questions. No one would believe Bael suddenly felt this way towards me, and my mistake would indeed be discovered.

Luckily, the two students don't seem to notice anything, and Bael inspects their potion quickly. After them, two more students appear, and on and on until the bell signaling the end of class chimes.

"Leave your potions on your desks, and I'll examine them after you leave. As for this weekend," he pauses, and everyone in the class holds their breath. "Enjoy it. Next week's lectures will be some of our hardest yet."

A rowdy cheer goes up as the other students grab their belongings and file out. I make no moves to leave. Watching the last students trickle out, I hear the door click firmly shut and fall into my discarded chair. Bael looks down at me, the air in the room shifting.

"That was close." I shake my head. "We have to be more discreet. It's easy to get, um, carried away."

Bael chuckles a rusty sound that tucks itself into my heart.

"Student-teacher relationships are frowned upon," he admits, leaning against the table. "I wouldn't want any ramifications happening this close to graduation."

I nod, suddenly feeling very tired. Bael looks at me closely and crosses his arms over his massive chest.

"I'm tempted to ask you to return after your period with Mistress Saege so we can begin your tutoring. However, I know it's the end of the week, and you surely have better plans."

I open my mouth but quickly shut it as I watch Bael kneel before me. His hands tangle with mine in my lap. Dark power flows from him, dancing with my own. If only this were real—no one has ever looked at me this way before.

"Darcee, I want—no, I need—to do this right. To court you properly as my people have done for centuries. I have to show you I can be worthy of you."

"Worthy of me? I'm not all that special," I say, swallowing.

His eyes harden slightly.

"There are no words that would do you justice. Never forget that."

I open my mouth to argue, but he continues.

"That is why I need to take this weekend to prepare. Tell me you want this, Darcee. There's no going back if you say yes. Be honest with me. Please."

I stare into his violet eyes and feel the weight of his promise pressing down on me. I am drowning in his scent and will greet death with a smile.

"Yes," I say. The selfish truth of it all is that I mean it. I'm not playing a game to appease the love potion. I mean it. That's what makes all of this so dangerous.

Hopefully, whatever needs to be planned won't be too elaborate, and it will become a distant, unpleasant memory for him once the potion fades.

"I'll begin tutoring you on Monday after class. I realize now you aren't much of a morning person." I meet his smile with one of my own. "There are three exams you need to retake. We should be able to accomplish them all before the grade submission deadline for graduation."

"Thank you, Bael. Truly."

A shiver goes through him as I say his name. Slowly, he rises to his feet, helping me out of the chair as he does. My head falls back as his fingers tuck a loose curl behind my ear. Gently, he skims over the shell, and now it's my turn to tremble.

"You are so beautiful. I thought it from the first moment I saw you."

I wrinkle my nose. "I had just had a charm blow up on me the period before. I was covered in day-old coffee grounds and chewed-up mint leaves."

Again, he laughs, a sound I'll never forget.

"A gallon of mud could be dropped on you, and you'd still be the loveliest woman I've ever laid eyes on."

"Don't manifest that for me," I say, even as my cheeks warm.

Pulling back, I collect my things from the desk. Bael observes each of my movements. I strode towards the door and finally looked at him over my shoulder.

"Have a nice weekend."

"You do the same, Darcee." A slight grin tugs at his lips. "I'll be watching."

I laugh and shake my head. The intensity in his gaze tells me he isn't kidding. The thrill that runs through me at the thought is delicious.

Dear Goddess, I am in so much trouble.

9

DARCEE

The following day, I arrive at Prue's door with a basket of baked goods resting in the crook of my elbow.

With a sharp knock, I hear her voice calling me from the other side. Prue's room has always been a collage of dark fabrics and sparkling tapestries. Her obsidian towers and black spell candles lay discarded atop her desk. An old leather-bound grimoire is open on her desk next to a small pot of ink—incense, and the smell of smoke swirls around me.

Along the far wall, Prue lies tucked into her purple velvet sheets. Next to her is a tired-looking Zander dressed in a wrinkled white shirt and linen pants. Dark circles are under his vibrant eyes, and his usually glowing brown skin has lost some of its luster. My heart gives a painful squeeze.

"Darcee," Prue says. "I'm happy to see you."

I raise the basket in my arms.

"I brought treats," I say lamely.

Zander rises from her side to take the basket from my hand.

"I'm so sorry," I tell him. "Truly."

The warlock shakes his head, his braids hitting along his shoulders.

"It's alright. Prue and I bear some of the burden in our haste to take it. We should've double-checked with you."

Zander settles the basket on the small table next to Prue, snagging a blueberry muffin for himself. He kisses her forehead softly, and I watch my friend practically melt. Their love is apparent; I can almost see it tethering them together.

"I'll give you two some privacy," he says, nodding at me as he slips from the room.

Once he is gone, Prue's face morphs into a conspiratorial smile.

"You're fully recovered, aren't you?" I ask.

She giggles.

"Nearly. I just love how much he's doting on me." Her eyes turn dreamy. "Even without the love potion, I've felt this shift between us. He's spent every waking moment with me—making sure I have everything I need—never leaving my side longer than necessary. And I have you to thank for it."

I meet her smile with one of my own.

"It's what I do best. Even when I mess up, love still finds a way."

"Speaking of," Prue says. Reaching beside her, she opens the table's top drawer and pulls out a small cloth bag. "Here."

Before she can hand it to me, I hold my hands and wave her off. Prue lets out an exasperated sigh.

"Darcee, take my coins. And don't tell me it's too much. You don't charge enough for your services."

I swallow. "It's not about the money. It's about bringing people together."

"And you, my selfless friend, have brought dozens of people together free of charge. Allow me, as your best friend, to pay you for guiding me toward the love of my life by helping secure your apothecary so that you may bring even more people together."

I take the bag from her and tuck it into my pocket. It is far too heavy, and Prue knows she's been too generous. Regardless, my friend is right: the price of my apothecary is staggering. I have enough to cover the rent for the first month. Buying it would be more financially sound, but I don't have enough for a down payment. However, through my hard work and dedication, I know I'll have people flocking to me from all over for my love readings.

I'm manifesting that, at least.

Besides, returning home is absolutely out of the question. With the apothecary, my living accommodations are included in the price. The small apartment above is nothing special, but I'd live in a run-down shed in the *Wicked Woods* before returning to my parents.

A cold sweat breaks out along my skin. Memories flash all more horrible than the last. The yelling, the isolation, the pain...Goddess, I need to stop, lest I won't sleep a wink tonight. No matter how much I wish things were different—and in moments of desperation, I feel myself reaching for them—my family will never accept me for who I am.

When will I ever make peace with that?

My sleep is already restless enough; I don't need to add my memories to it. Last night, I was consumed with thoughts of Bael. In dreams, I reached for him and felt the weight of his body against mine. The warmth of his hands caressed me as his deep voice spoke soft words of adoration. I had awoken sweating through my nightgown. Throwing open the windows to my room and letting in the chilly night air had barely helped.

His purple eyes watched me, feeling like a physical touch along my body. It was as if he was calling to me in my mind— urging me to join him in his dreams. When I woke again, my sheets were tangled around my waist, and my heart was pounding.

Even now, I can feel him watching me. Calling out to me and—

"You seem distracted," Prue comments.

I glance up at her and offer a sheepish smile.

"Lots on my mind," I say. "Graduation."

"Speaking of, did you ever decide what you would do about the High Warlock?"

I still at her question.

"What—uh, what do you mean?"

Prue's dark brows lower. "Your grade. Did you ask him for help like I suggested?"

I nearly sag with relief.

"Oh! Yes, I did. He's going to let me retake the exams."

My friend's mouth parted slightly.

"Really?"

I nod. "The prospect of me failing and having to repeat the course was probably enough incentive for him to let me try again. Spare us both the agony of being around each other any longer."

"Hmm. Well, that's good. Zander mentioned that he seemed different when he saw him yesterday evening. Maybe the end of the semester has improved his mood."

"Different, how?" I ask.

Prue waves dismissively and plucks a piece of coffee cake from the basket.

"Zander said he seemed lighter. Whatever that means." She shrugs, cracking open the baked good and watching the steam rise. "I'm glad we only missed one class. I'll be playing catch-up before our trip next weekend. It's good that we had our little mishap with the sleeping potion now and not next week. I don't think Zander would've taken missing out on *the Bog* too well."

I wrinkle my nose. I had nearly forgotten all about our end-of-the-year trip to *the Bog*. We were supposed to use our field skills to secure one of the rare ingredients needed for our final exam. Our final test would be crafting the *Dead Man's Serum*, a highly valuable and convoluted potion. If I can improve my previous exam grades, failing the potion won't ruin my ability to pass.

"I hate that place," I mutter.

"But an overnight trip off school property? Now that sounds like fun."

"Only because you'll be sneaking into Zander's tent," I laugh.

Her eyes glint as she wiggles her brows at me.

An overnight trip with Bael. Goddess, that is an unnecessary risk. Hopefully, by that point, the potion will have faded significantly. If a week goes past with no change, I'll craft him an antidote myself. Hopefully, it won't come to that. I'll just have to keep my wits about me until then.

Having heady dreams about him isn't helping the situation.

Neither is the ease in which it is to flirt with him. There is a wretched, reckless part of me that longs to tease him as if we are true lovers. After all, that's one of the most exciting parts of being in love—the beginning, where everything is new and you can learn about each other. Bael seems cold and standoffish, yet the heat I feel from him sets me on fire. I like playing with it —tempting him even if I shouldn't.

Again, I hope that if he sees me as an eager participant, he will be too embarrassed to broach the subject again once the potion fades. He will end it, and we will never speak of it or each other again.

Even as I think it, I can't help but feel a pang of sadness.

If I am already going this mushy over a few stolen touches and hushed confessions, what will I be like when he begins properly courting me? What will that even entail? I'll need to recenter myself this weekend. I cannot afford to make this situation any worse by losing myself to the power of the love potion.

Rising on shaky legs, I lean down and kiss Prue brow.

"I have to go check on a few things. I'll come by again tomorrow."

"I'd love that," she sighs.

No sooner do I turn from the bed than Zander pushes into the room as if waiting for the moment he could return. He gives me a rushed farewell before settling in at Prue's side. I watch them for a moment. The tethers of their souls are fusing— strengthening.

Jealousy and happiness course through me, and I wonder what it is like to find that. Bael's perceived love for me isn't real, but it's easy to pretend it is. Especially as I take in the look in Zander's eyes and realize with a heavy heart that Bael looks at me the same way.

Soon enough, contempt will return to his violet eyes when he stares at me. I will not allow myself to be swept up by my spell, even if that is easier said than done.

10

———

THE HIGH WARLOCK

He lies tormented in his bed.

The whispers from beyond the veil are silent for the moment. The male they normally pester is awash in his madness. He has managed not to alert her of his presence for two days. Even as he crept down hallways after her sweet scent, he transformed into a raven and settled on her window sill, watching for hours as she flitted about her room.

He remained her silent watcher as the sun began to set. He flew off when she started to change for bed. Any glimpse of her naked skin would send him deeper into his hysteria. The stalking was deplorable enough.

He stayed until exhaustion began to weigh him down and returned to his cottage.

How will he keep himself in check when he sees her again? He doesn't know, but he will—he'll do this properly and earn her affection. For now, he settles for the version of her in his dreams.

Pink curls tickle his chin. Small hands are warm and seeking as they glide over his skin. They skim lower, searching for the hardness that's only ever formed for her. Once he earns her affection, he will give in to his completion for the first time. Only with her—she is it for him.

His plan is already in motion. Knowing he will see her again soon, his body surrenders to slumber again. Warm hands pull him down into its waiting depth, and magenta eyes see into his soul.

11

———

DARCEE

I did not know what it was, but I knew who had sent it.

It appeared in the center of my room just as dawn was breaking. The soft glow woke me up, and now I find myself face to face with the largest crystal I have ever seen. It sits in the center of my room, refracting the morning light. My walls are awash in rainbow-colored light beams as the stone glimmers.

The obsidian block pulses with power. Its opaque surface is pristine—smooth and round—and seems otherworldly. Its dark color contrasts sharply with the light pastels my room is filled with. Tentatively, I crawl out of bed and take a step towards it. The sun has now fully risen. Its golden light seeps through my windows and lands squarely on the stone.

There is silence for a moment—my beating heart roars in my ears. Then, a loud crack ripples through the room. I gasp as a deep gash forms at the top of the crystal. It spreads like a spider's web down the sides—snapping and breaking until it falls open.

Inside is a swath of amethyst. The jagged edges of the shattered stones stick up like broken teeth. The sunlight pours over each crystal, casting my room in glowing, purple light. More cracking echoes around me as I watch the amethyst take shape. With a gentle hum, it moves of its own accord, rearranging into a series of flowers made from the hard crystal.

My eyes narrow in on the massive bouquet and the lone piece of parchment resting atop the still blooms. It is enclosed with a wax seal depicting a raven resting next to a skull—Bael's seal.

Power tickles my fingertips as I reach for it. I can hear voices whispering in the room around me—spurning me on to take it. Cool air pours from the mess of stones. My bare arms prickling with goosebumps. Holding the note, I take a deep breath and snap the wax.

Bael's elegant script greets me:

'Your beauty is bewitching, and your soul is kind. Please allow me the honor of calling you mine. You have haunted the hidden depths of my soul. I yearn for your touch that would make me whole. I'll wait forever at the mercy of your whims, longing for the day I can hold you in my limbs.'

An infectious giggle bursts out of me. Goddess, he is so cute—and a little cheesy, but that makes my heart melt further. I tuck the note against my chest and close my eyes. It even smells faintly of him. I inhale greedily.

It's my first love note ever, and it's from Bael. Who would've thought? The reality of why he sent all this to me threatens to ruin the moment, but I won't let it. I need to play along and to do that, I must embrace this courting ritual. It'll be nice to pretend it's real for a little while.

Opening my eyes, I reach for an empty box on my desk and lay the note in it. I'll discard all the evidence once this is over.

Another powerful hum cuts through the air. The crystal flowers begin to shimmer and shake, glowing with a new intensity that leads to a riotous explosion of colors. Purple glitter dances through the air in a misty cloud before the crystal bouquet transforms into one of real lilacs.

Their fragrance perfumes my tiny dorm room. The plants begin to sprawl out into a magnificent display. Tears burn my eyes as I touch the soft petals. They are my favorite flowers. How could he possibly have known that? It must've been a lucky guess.

Lifting the blooms from the crystal, I deposit them into a large glass vase and fill it with new moon water; the petals glimmer and swell. I stare at them as warmth spreads throughout my body.

My peaceful morning is interrupted by a sharp knock at my door. Hastily grabbing a robe, I throw it on and open the door. I'm expecting to find someone—secretly hoping that it's Bael. However, when my eyes are greeted by nothing but an empty hallway, I'm immediately confused. That is, until the mouthwatering scent of chocolate hits me.

Glancing down, I'd recognize the familiar glossy black box from the local bakery anywhere. Taking it back into my room, I settle it atop my desk and pluck the note from the top.

Something sweet is written in Bael's script.

Taking off the top, a fresh wave of butter, sugar, and chocolate perfection invades my lungs. The glossy, golden brown tops of the pastries sparkle up at me. Licking my lips, I pick one up and bite into it. The crunch gives way to a buttery, soft perfection, and sweet chocolate coats my tongue.

I moan at the taste. They're still warm.

Collecting his second note, I put it in the box with the other one and secure the lid. I don't need anyone discovering these while I'm out. Taking another bite of the pastry, I stare out at the castle's grounds through my window. *I'm in danger*, I think.

The notion sends a delicious thrill through me, but I can't bring myself to care.

THAT AFTERNOON, I find myself in Mistress Saege's room earlier than usual.

Due to my new tutoring lessons, I switched my hour with Saege to my free period before necromancy. She did not question the change. Merely gave me a pile of grimoires she needed my help sorting through and cataloging. After I finished, I began working on my grimoire and recording the sleeping potion I made.

While it was administered to the wrong person, it worked remarkably. It could be helpful to me in the future. I dip my pen in the ink pot and scroll on the worn piece of parchment. Off to the side, Mistress Saege is behind her desk with a few vials of brightly colored liquid floating around her. Her lace bell sleeves drag along the surface of her desk as she waves her wand delicately.

"How was your weekend, my dear?" she asks casually.

Oh, you know, I just have a centuries-old necromancy professor sending me gifts because he believes himself in love with me. I accidentally slipped him a love potion that will no doubt lead to my expulsion. How was yours?

Instead of saying all of that, I give a noncommittal shrug.

"Quiet, mainly. Gave me time to make more rose water."

Mistress Saege nods, but her eyes have a conspiratorial glimmer to them.

"Marius was asking about you on Friday," she says casually.

I sketch a brow. "Who's playing love witch now?"

The wrinkles around her eyes deepen as she grins.

"I don't know what you're talking about, my dear."

Shaking my head, I let out a soft chuckle.

"Marius doesn't want me. He thinks he does because I'm the only woman at this school who rejected him." I gently close my grimoire. "I decided I was bored of him first, and he can't stand it."

"But you liked him?" she pries.

Mistress Saege has always felt like the big sister I never had. I enjoy our open dialogue. I've confided in her more times than I can count, and each time, her advice has been—well—sage.

"For a time," I say softly. "Though—"

A large crash sends me nearly flying out of my seat. The vials Saege was levitating fell to her desk but luckily remained whole. I whip my head to the side, and my breath is stolen.

Bael is here. How had I not heard him come in? His hair gleams in the light. Violet eyes meet mine, and their intensity causes my blood to heat. Full gray lips are set in their usual straight line, but there is something sensual about them now. His black cape spills behind him.

A pile of broken glass rests at his feet—one of Saege's unused large spell jars.

"My apologies," he says, voice low. It feels like fingers gliding over my skin. "I bumped into it."

His eyes never leave mine even as Mistress Saege rises and comes to stand between us. I lick my suddenly dry lips and remain stuck to my chair.

"That's quite alright," Saege says, waving her hand and removing the glass. "I hadn't even heard you enter."

As if remembering himself, his spine straightens. He nods at me politely.

"Miss Thistle," he says before fixing his stare on the other witch. "The Head Mistress said you had something for me."

Saege's eyebrows lower before her eyes fly open with a nod.

"Oh, yes. Yes! Thank you for coming on such short notice. I know you have a class coming up. Let me grab it from my office. I'll only be a moment."

With that, Saege turns into a swirl of white fabric. We both watch her take the spiral staircase to her office on the above floor. The door shuts with a gentle click and the air around us shifts. His eyes devour me whole as he prowls closer. My breathing turns ragged, and my frilly pink top and skirt suddenly seem too stifling.

His scent hits me, and a fresh wave of desire rolls through me. Have I always felt this way towards him? Was it buried underneath disdain because I thought he hated me? While a spell manufactures his desire, it's becoming alarmingly apparent mine is all too real.

I clear my throat.

"Thank you for the flowers. They're beautiful. And the pastries were delicious." Heat engulfs my cheeks. "But the love notes were my favorite. No one's ever given me one before."

His pupils nearly blot out all traces of purple.

"Good," he says simply.

My lips twitch

"Possessive."

His hands come down on either side of me at the desk. Leaning down, I have to tilt my face to meet his gaze. The warmth radiating from him licks my skin.

"When it comes to you? Always."

A soft moan leaves me as I rise in my seat. What is this? I've never felt desire like this—raw and unchecked. It moves me towards him and eradicates all thoughts of self-preservation. There's playing along, and then there's wishing he'd meet my mouth with his.

Which is what I'm actively doing.

"Bael," I whisper, licking my lips.

His pained groan is music to my ears. Our mouths drift closer, and I feel his breath against my mouth. That's it—just a bit closer and—

"Found it!" Saege calls from above.

We spring apart, and Bael takes two large steps from my desk. The older witch descends the stairs quickly. A white envelope extended towards Bael. Her eyes glance between us, saying nothing for a moment before nodding.

"Raen said you know more about this than anyone."

Bael opens it and reads the letter before tucking it in his pocket.

"Tell the Head Mistress I'll look into it."

A shrill bell cuts through the room. On wobbly legs, I rise and collect my books. I say my goodbyes to Saege, who looks at me strangely. Her eyes drift to Bael, who has come to stand beside me.

"I'll escort you to class, Miss Thistle."

I nod and follow him to the door.

"See you tomorrow!" I call over my shoulder.

The sea of students swallows us up. Having Bael at my side causes the others to keep their distance. I can still feel his heat rolling towards me in waves. His scent of smoke, earth, and midnight air overwhelms me. I want to drink it and let it become a part of me.

I am just as affected as him. It's impossible—but these feelings are strong.

Did Mistress Saege sense something between us, or am I just paranoid? I can't be sure. The burning intensity in Bael's gaze is hard to miss. If you are looking for it, the signs are evident in the attention he pays me.

A strong hand tugs on my sleeve, and I look up at Bael. He nods towards a desolate corridor off to the side.

"This way. I know a shortcut."

I follow his tall frame into the quiet hall. The golden afternoon sun streams in from the window off to the side. We stand facing a brick wall, and Bael reaches out. His palm glows with purple fire as he presses a brick. There is a soft groan and then a symphony of clicks as the bricks rumble open. Dust falls between them as they peel apart, revealing a hidden passageway.

My laugh is one of surprise. Bael extends his hand towards the darkness.

"After you."

I duck into the dim corridor—the only light comes from the staircase above and a lone torch on the wall. The floor is uneven, and my heel gets trapped under my cape. I slide—losing my footing—my books toppling to the floor with a slam. I brace myself for impact until I feel warm hands grabbing my waist.

Bael holds me upright and slowly walks me back against the near wall. The opening closes with a rumble, encasing us in silent darkness. My breathing turns sharper as I stare at him. The dim light casts his face in jagged shadows. It makes him look dangerous. A fresh wave of desire rolls through me, turning me hot and wet between my thighs.

Goddess, this is not good. My hands curl into the front of his shirt and pull him closer. His hands begin to roam over my body. Violet's eyes search mine, and I nod, encouraging him to touch me more. Our laborious breaths are the only sound in the corridor.

He presses against me. The muscles of his chest and back are taut. My hands slip under his shirt and pull him even deeper into me. That seeking hardness presses against my stomach, and I moan. He growls, his head falling to my shoulder.

"Darcee," he snarls. I whimper as his nose skims up my neck. "I was meant to do this properly. To take things slow."

His hands drift higher up my ribs. Thumbs graze the underside of my breasts through my bra. After a few more minutes of touching, I could climax.

"It's hard when you are so tempting," he continues. "Everything is so hard."

"Bael," I whisper. I need any sort of relief I can find.

"You are a madness—my madness. One I'm more than willing to succumb to."

"Yes," I whisper.

His lips skim the skin of my throat before he pulls back. Our hands rove over each other, but it never goes further. Our movements are thoughtful, as if committing each other to memory.

This is wrong—he's my teacher and under the effects of a love potion—but I want him all the same. If he said the word, I'd happily strip out of my clothes and let him have his way with me. Something that would make this whole situation worse.

Thankfully, he doesn't ask. The bell rings again overhead, and we both need the wake-up call. With one last deep inhale at my neck, Bael pulls back. My chest rises and falls as I watch him stoop down and collect my books. Dusting them off, he hands them out to me. My hands shake as I take them.

He nods at the stone stairs above us.

"You go up first. I'll follow in a few minutes."

I nod and shakily take the stairs. The world around me is a blur. Worry tickles icy claws down my spine. How will I survive our first tutoring session without taking things too far?

When it comes to Bael, I am just as much at his mercy as he is at the mercy of my love potion.

12

DARCEE

Necromancy class had always been a dull, frustrating affair.

The concepts did not agree with me, and the professor leading the class held unbridled disdain for me. Now, that couldn't be farther from the truth. Before, I sometimes found it difficult to pay attention because of the material being taught. Now, I'm having difficulty focusing as I watch Bael confidently glide around the room, instructing us to cast a summoning circle without being tapped beyond the veil.

My mind is filled with the memory of Bael's strong hands tracing along my body. How warm and hard he had been pressing against me—our shared breath—the delicious secrecy of being with him. Our relationship is wrong—unethical for many reasons—yet my desire for him was rapidly increasing by the moment. That love potion I gave him must have been my most potent brew yet, even I feel under its thrall.

As he highlights the difference between black and pink salt, I watch his slender muscles flex under his shirt as he writes. A hot thrill goes through me, and I wonder again if this attraction to him was always there on my end. We wouldn't be the first opposites to attract—I have brought together dozens of people who seem at odds with one another only to end up being a perfect match.

Perhaps buried beneath all that disdain was a kernel of my true feelings. I had always wanted to impress him. Other professors had dismissed me, but Bael's cut deeper for some reason. His assertion that I wasn't taking the course seriously ruffled me and spurned me to try harder, even if it was to no avail.

His eyes scan the room, connecting with mine for a moment before moving on. Awareness spreads throughout my body, tingling in my fingers. The heat in his gaze makes it easy to forget this isn't real. While my emotions are genuine, his will begin to wane this week. They have to. Until then, heavy petting and constant flirting will have to suffice.

After that, I'll be gone and never see him again. All of this will fade into an unpleasant memory for him, and he'll be none the wiser about how it came about in the first place.

Opening a leatherbound textbook on his desk, he reads off a passage in a deep voice. Goddess, he is handsome. I can admit that now—though some part of me has always thought so. The fullness of his lips was in sharp contrast to the harshness of his jaw. His purple eyes glowed under dark, arched eyebrows. Pointed ears poked out from beneath his swath of black hair.

Even without his gray skin, no one would ever consider Bael human. The depth in his gaze and the way he moves with predatory grace indicates he is not of this world. Those eyes fixate on mine again, and a fresh flush breaks across my cheeks. I have to rub my thighs together and soothe the dull ache there. His lips twitch as if he knows, but he merely continues reading, his words never faltering.

If I am becoming his madness, he is undoubtedly already mine. I've never felt this desire before. If he doesn't touch me again, soon I'll perish. It was never like this with Marius—or any of the others I had dabblings with over the years. Part of this could be due to the dry spell I've been having. How long has it been since I last had sex? A year, maybe longer.

I hadn't noticed the time between now and my last tryst with a fourth-year charms student. It seems my body knows it hasn't found release at the hands of another in some time. All that pent-up desire flows through me unencumbered, demanding I submit. I should find another for a quick romp, but the thought of anyone besides Bael repulses me.

It is futile, seeing as I can never have him in that way—especially not now.

Therefore, I will deny myself. For a moment, I wondered if we could try again once the potion was out of his system. The thought is pointless—when Bael shakes off this stupor, he'll never wish to see me again. If he does, it will only be to punish me.

The bell rings and cuts through my inappropriate thoughts. All at once, the students around me begin moving, writing down the mountain of spellwork Bael has assigned for the evening. Prue slips her belongings into her bag at my side and looks at me expectantly.

"Zander is going to help me get caught up on the class I missed last week. You wanna join?"

I hope my grin is convincing.

"I can't. Ba—The High Warlock is—"

I'm spared from answering further when Zander appears. His skin has once again returned to its healthy glow. The darkness under his eyes is barely a whispered smudge.

"Ready to go?" he asks Prue, nodding down at me in greeting.

"Sure," she says, eyeing me momentarily before slinging her bag over her shoulder. "See you later, Dar."

They both leave with the remaining stranglers. Awareness prickles my skin as I watch the last student slip out the door.

The air around me is stifling, and every sense in my body is heightened. I turn towards the front of the room, where Bael leans against his large wooden desk. His arms are casually crossed over his chest, and his long leg is tucked over the other.

We stare at each other for several moments, saying nothing and everything simultaneously. It is intoxicating to be looked at this way—like I am the center of his world. My legs clench together once more. The bare skin of my thighs is highly sensitive.

Once more, the side of his mouth kicks up as he waves a hand. The door to the room locks with finality. I remain rooted to my chair as he prowls closer. His graceful movements cause my heart to pound.

"We shouldn't have any interruptions," he says. His voice is soft and rough at the same time.

"Good." I swallow loudly.

His booted feet gently click along the wooden floor as he walks closer to me. The scent of smoke and earth invades my lungs and worsens my ache. When he reaches my desk, his palms fall to the smooth surface on either side of me. Our position mirrors how we were in Mistress Saege's class. I stare up at him, taking in his formidable figure.

The top button of his shirt has come undone, revealing more of his muscular gray skin. It is unmarred and seems impossibly soft. I'd love to trace the opening with my fingers—my tongue. Bael breathes heavily, his face lowering closer to mine. Our mouths are mere inches apart. To kiss him would be dangerous, and yet I feel my mouth tipping up higher to do just that.

"Do you," Bael pauses, swallowing loudly, "have any idea how beautiful you are?"

The words caress me—my mouth parts with a soft sigh.

"Do you know how hard it is for me?" he continues. "To sit

up there and teach a lesson when you are sitting here tempting me."

"Bael," I whisper, licking my lips.

"Is it wrong that I've wanted you like this countless times? I've been close—so close—to dismissing everyone but you so I could have you all to myself."

I inhale sharply at his confession. His eyes burn brighter—madness threading through his purple irises.

"Does the knowledge of my desire frighten you, little witch?"

A hot shiver goes through me. Once more, my string is being pulled by an unseen force, and I'm powerless to fight it. My hand comes down on top of his, tracing the back of it. Skimming over his hard knuckles and veins, I bite my lip and drown in his stare.

"No," I say, and it is the truth. "I only wish you had said something sooner."

His low growl is music to my ears. It's easy to flirt when it feels real to me. If I were an ethical witch, I'd call this all off. I'd risk giving him an antidote to end his affliction sooner, but I'm not a good witch. It's selfish and wrong, but this may be the only chance to indulge in this buried fantasy of Bael before I leave.

We will not take things too far—sex is firmly off the table while he is under the effects of a love potion. However, flirting, touching, and, Goddess, spare me a stolen kiss or two is fair game. I need to experience it—him—just once before I graduate. That way, I can leave this place with no regrets.

I want him, and he needs me while the potion is still this potent.

His large hand lifts from under mine, rising to tuck a loose curl behind my ear. My heart races as his fingertips explore the shell of my ear before skimming over my cheek and the bridge of my nose. My face warms under his stare. Tucking his finger underneath my chin, he tilts my face higher. My eyes flutter shut as his head lowers. His nose nestles between my shoulder and neck, inhaling deeply.

He drags it along his fingers' path, and I wait to feel his lips on mine. The anticipation is delicious agony. My hands clench the desk before me as his lips skim over my ear. A delightful shiver runs down my spine.

"As tempting as you are, I will not use these tutoring sessions to have my way with you. You deserve to be properly courted, but more than that, I am your professor first. Improving your grade is my primary concern when you are here. Things will remain professional, you have my word." I feel him smile against my ear. "Even as it's taking all my restraint not to toss you up on my desk and strip you out of that little skirt."

Before I can stop it, a moan slips out of my mouth. Bael pulls back, his eyes dark and wild. His voice is uneven when he speaks again.

"I've already set out your first exam on poisons and elixirs in my office. We will begin in there."

With a wave of his hand, the books and notebooks strewn across my desk levitate, as does the bag hanging from my chair. They float through the air to a silver metal door behind his chalkboards. It squeaks open, and warm orange light spills across the stone floor.

Bael takes a step back and gestures towards it.

"After you."

Rising on shaking knees, I gather my discarded cloak and fold it in my arms over my chest. I walk towards his office, his large body close behind mine. Once inside, the sight steals my breath.

A large hearth with a roaring fire snaps and crackles but puts off no eat. Hundreds of tall black and white candles make up the warm ambiance. A large maple wood desk sits in front of a high-back leather chair. Various papers and pots of ink are littered across its surface. On the walls hang various dissected bugs and plants. Five large bookcases take up any open free space—each nearly bursting with the amount of volumes stuffed on each shelf.

I glance at him over my shoulder, a smile on my lips.

"It smells like you in here."

A shiver rolls through him, but he says nothing. I sink into the plush leather chair across from his desk. The cool material tickles my bare skin. I note that, with some interest, he doesn't shut the door.

He settles in across from me, and I realize how deep I've fallen into all this. I'm hanging on his every word—every touch. If he breathed on me correctly, I would climax from it. This is wrong, and I don't want it to stop. Ever.

Bael's large hand runs over the parchment before him. My first exam—the only one I did seemingly decent on—now glares up at me with its barely passing grade. The High Warlock flips through it momentarily, a muscle in his jaw ticking before glancing up at me again.

"What do you remember from this lesson?"

Heat erupts on my cheeks, and it's a fight not to drop his stare.

"Very little," I admit.

Bael nods once, and with a wave of his hand, my notebook flops open to a blank page. A pen with a fresh pot of ink slides towards me.

"Then let us start at the beginning, yes?"

I nod eagerly and snatch up my pen.

"To understand death, we must first learn its causes. While it seems scary to some, it is a part of life. What is given must always be returned. But how? Time, of course, takes many. Illness, as well. But then there are more measured means of inflicting death that we have control over. Let's go over a few of those now..."

I hang on to Bael's every word. Somehow, now that he's only speaking to me, they seem to have a more substantial impact. He talks slower, rephrasing things in ways so I comprehend. After a few minutes of listening to his lecture, I understand better than ever before.

Not to mention, his authoritative teaching voice is turning me obscenely slippery between my thighs. Goddess help me.

As Bael continues, one thing becomes painfully clear to me: It won't be easy to walk away from him at the end. I have a sinking suspicion that once all this is said and done, doing so might just break my heart.

13

———

THE HIGH WARLOCK

After an hour, it is clear that necromancy and Darcee will never agree.

That matters little to him. He would gladly spend countless more hours together in his office going over the same subjects—explaining and reexplaining things—until she understood. This is a clear show of favoritism, and as an upstanding professor who takes his job seriously, he should feel ashamed. However, as he watches Darcee's cheeks deepen with color as the subject matter finally clicks for her, he can't bring himself to care.

Their whole dynamic is inappropriate, but he always knew it would be. In a few weeks, none of this will matter. They'll no longer have to hide and dance around their connection.

Well, what he hopes is their connection. Surely, she is not immune to it. The desire is strong enough to burn him alive. He aches with it. Every moment in her presence lowers his defenses, and the primal part of him grows more assertive. He would've taken her in Saege's room—would take her now in this one, but he vowed to show restraint. They can be together that way once he has fully won her affection.

For now, he has a job to do.

Even if it is impossible not to be tempted by her, the madness stretches as he stares at Darcee. Her short skirt ends midthigh, showing off a creamy expanse of pale skin before the tops of her boots begin. Her white shirt is poking out from underneath, a few buttons undone to highlight the small swells of her breast. They rise and fall with each deep breath.

He remembers being in the darkened corridor with her. They had been so close to his mouth—a forbidden temptation. The feel of her against his palms had nearly made him lose control. Darcee was all soft curves and even softener sighs. It had tempted the parts of him he'd kept buried—the ones inherited from his father.

Once he is satisfied with her comprehension, the lesson ends. Carefully, she slides her books and parchment away before looking at him again. Her eyes dance with mischief. Dark pink lips pull into a grin. The High Warlock curls his shaking hands in on themselves to stop himself from snatching her up and carrying her away.

"You did well," he says. His voice sounds strange to his ears.

Her grin deepens.

"Maybe I was just needing some private tutoring this whole time." Magenta eyes turn thoughtful. "I hadn't even thought to ask."

He nods. The shame at how he let her struggle in class creeps up his neck.

"I was unfair to you, little witch. I'll never stop apologizing for it."

Her small hand slides towards him, resting atop his trembling one. The slight touch sets him on fire. Desire roars in his blood, and his whole body hardens.

"We have been unfair to each other."

White teeth sink into her full lower lip. How badly he wishes to taste her—to have her as he's always dreamed.

"Thank you," she whispers. "Words don't seem enough for what you have done for me."

The High Warlock's nostrils flare. The scent of lilacs and sweet honey invade his lungs. His cock hardens into steel, a new sensation only brought upon by her. He cannot give in to his desire—not yet. However, what she is offering....

"I didn't bring you in here for that. You don't owe me anything for helping you."

A lovely blush breaks out along her cheeks.

"I know," she says softly, rising from her seat.

He holds his breath as she rounds his desk. Pushing back, he turns in his chair to face her. The soft leather groans as his fingers dig into it.

"That makes me want to do this even more."

Before he can utter a word, every thought empties from his head as he watches Darce—lovely and pink—crawl into his lap. Her thighs go on either side of his legs as she settles against him. Warm and soft. Curly pink hair tickles his cheeks.

He is losing the battle of keeping his hands at his side, fighting to resist her temptation. Darcee is unburdened, and her small hands raise to cup his cheeks. She holds him for balance but also to position his face just right. Her pink tongue licks her lips before her eyes flutter shut.

Slowly, her face drifts towards his. He could stop this at any time and demand that they wait so that he may court her properly. Yet, he has denied himself for so long. Why stop when she wants this just as much as he does?

Her soft lips press against his, and everything changes. It is all the confirmation he needs. His blood roars, his muscles tighten, and his cock presses against the front of his trousers. A low snarl gathers in his chest.

With shaking hands, he crushes her firmly against him. Her small breasts press into his chest, and she moans into their kiss.

His madness has just reached a new level, and one undeniable truth pumps through him.

Now that he's tasted her, he's never letting her go.

14

———

DARCEE

In all honesty, I hadn't meant to kiss him.

At least not this soon. A stolen kiss here or there a few days from now would've been enough. Something chaste before the potion was out of his system. It would make the situation awkward enough for Bael never to bring it up again, and I could graduate in peace.

Instead, I crawled into his lap and am now trying to eat him alive. The kiss is not as chaste as I planned it to be. The first brushing of his lips against mine had set me on fire. The High Warlock tastes of mint and spice. His smell wraps around me like an embrace. My hands slide from his cheek to tunnel into the silk strands of his dark hair. The kiss breaks for a moment to allow me to breathe, and then our lips are together again.

Low growls and groans slip between his teeth. I gasp as his hands dig into my back, locking me to him. Bael wastes no time in slipping his tongue into my mouth. I moan against it, loving the silky feel as ours tangle together.

It is his fault, really. He just had to be so handsome. His commanding voice had worked me into a state. He had been patient and compassionate with me, which snapped my restraint. I had to taste him—if only this once. It's been a long time since I've been kissed, and all of that need is rolling through me, focused singularly on him.

Surprisingly, Bael doesn't kiss with any real finesse of a practiced lover. His mouth is hungry against mine, but there is no teasing or playing. His kisses are earnest, and that causes more arousal to rush through me. His wandering hands are just as thoughtful as they use my hips to work against him.

His seeking hardness is rampant between my spread thighs. He growls against me, his head falling back against the chair. I writhe on him again and moan at the delicious friction. Hands skim up my back before tangling in my hair. He pulls me to him with a gentle tug, and we resume kissing.

I teach him exactly what I like. The frenzy of our kiss slows as his tongue works with mine before retreating. His mouth drifts lower to kiss down my neck, biting and sucking as he goes. One hand remains in my hair, but the other travels to my backside. Warm fingers fall to the back of my thighs and inch up my bare skin.

"Bael," I sigh, his fingers dangerously close to the one place I need him but can't allow him.

I don't stop him, though, wicked thing that I am. They skim up my leg and under my skirt. Bael sighs against my neck, his warm breath tickling me.

"I can feel just how much you're enjoying this," he purrs.

My vision goes blurry as his finger slips under the silk strap of my panties along my hip. Our mouths reunite in a clash of tongues and teeth. My own hands move, seeking their forbidden treasure. I skim them down his chest as he licks along my jaw. His head nuzzles under my chin, and his lips press between my breasts.

Not to be outdone, my hands find the waistband of his pants. This is wrong, but I can't help myself. The desire is pouring off him in waves. My fingers barely creep below the top of his pants when his hand wraps around mine.

Through heavy-lidded eyes and ragged breath, I watch him shake his head—only once. His breathing is labored as we stay tangled together. His hand slides out from under my clothes and rests firmly on my hip, slowing my movements.

"Not yet," he rasps.

I can't hide my pout. In these situations, I'm used to getting my way. Bael chuckles darkly before laying another kiss on me.

"As I said before, little witch, I do not want to rush things between us. There is still much I have planned to woo you."

My lips twitch.

"I do so like to be wooed," I say softly, resting my forehead against his.

His smile is brilliant, and I know I'm the only person who's ever seen it—all because of a lie. The truth of our relationship slams into me. With the frenzy of the kiss cooling, the reality of the situation looms between us. I slide off his lap and tug my clothes back into place.

Goddess, what is wrong with me? Have I no care? Can't I show an ounce of control for even a moment? With this level of encouragement, the potion's effects will only linger. They could intensify if I'm not careful.

At this moment, I make a silent pack. Once Bael has helped me retake all my tests, I will make him an antidote. If the potion has not begun to wane, I will end this by graduation.

I slip on my cloak while Bael picks up my bag, and we exit into the main room. My face heats at the look of his swollen lips. Mine feel just as tender, and I'm sure my hair is in a state. I need to get a better handle on my feelings, if not for him than for myself. Even though it shouldn't have happened, I can't regret my kiss with Bael. It was the best one I've ever had.

Outside in the main room, the sun is nearly set. Streaks of

gold and pink decorate the desolate classroom. In the evenings, the castle is comfortingly still.

"Would you like me to walk you back to your dorm?" Bael asks.

I smile up at him but shake my head. Taking my bag from him, I toss it over my shoulder.

"We're supposed to be discreet, remember?"

Bael chuckles, his thumb raising to glide along my lower lip.

"You look thoroughly kissed," he whispers.

A fresh blush erupts on my cheeks as he bends down and meets my mouth in a chaste brush of our lips. It is over far too soon, and I hunger for more instantly. My panties are a sodden mess.

With a wave of his hand, the door to the room unlocks with a loud clang.

"Are you up for another session tomorrow? I threw a lot at you today." His eyes darken. "In more than one way."

"I'm ready for more," I assure him.

Bael nods. "Good. We'll need to work fast to finish the first and second exams before the class trip to *the Bog* this weekend."

I can't help but wrinkle my nose.

"I hate that place. It's scary out there."

"You know I'll keep you safe."

"Hmm. You promise?"

Bael chuckles again, his body inching closer to mine.

"If you think I'll be able to let you out of my sight for a second y—"

The door to the room groans open, and we jump apart. Standing at the threshold is Mistress Romina. Her shock is palpable. Her dark eyes look between us before her red-painted mouth settles into a hardline. Her hairstyle is as severe as the look she's leveling me with.

"Miss Thistle," she says stiffly—eyes narrowing. "High

Warlock, I didn't know you were busy. We usually meet at this time."

An ugly, oily emotion coats my tongue, and I dare a glance at Bael. I have no right to feel jealous. What if he does like Romina, and I ruined it all because of my potion? I think back to their body language at the equinox party. She was interested, but it was clearly one-sided. Still, maybe something would've blossomed between them if it weren't for me. Once I'm gone, they'll find their way back to each other.

I open my mouth to respond, but Bael beats me to it.

"Miss Thistle was requiring extra guidance before the end of the semester. She was just on her way out."

I stare at Bael, his surly mask firmly back in place. He only allows me to glimpse his smile and easy nature. That shouldn't please me as much as it does. Romina's mouth pinches around the corner, but she says nothing.

"Thank you for your help, High Warlock," I say as evenly as possible.

I switch places with Romina, who shuffles through the door effortlessly. She moves around Bael easily, and a fresh wave of jealousy rolls through me. I dare glance back, but they are already discussing as the door falls shut.

What is the nature of their relationship? How often do they meet? What do they discuss? These questions plague me as I enter the dining hall. I snag a few pieces of chicken and some roasted root vegetables before they close.

I quickly eat my dinner and return to my dorm room.

Once I shut and lock the door behind me, I sit at the edge of my bed and unzip my boots. Was there ever a better feeling than taking off your shoes after a long day? Yes—Bael's kisses. I'd wear my highest pair of heels until my feet bled for just one taste of his mouth again.

I laugh at myself. I sound ridiculous.

Hanging my cloak on the peg by the door, I'm tempted to

crawl into bed fully clothed when there is a cawing at my window. A lone raven sits on the sill, a small letter clasped in its beak. The wax seal on the front makes my heart race.

Pushing open the glass window, I pluck the note from his beak and offer him a pumpkin seed as a reward. He flutters away on delicate wings. Walking over to my desk in a daze, I stare at the lone triangle with a 'T' resting in the center cast in silver wax—my family seal.

With trembling hands, I snap it and quickly read my father's familiar script. Bile races up my throat, and tears burn in my eyes at the callous words. I was foolish for reaching out to them. Why do I always do that? I thought maybe enough time had passed with me gone—that things could be different. Now I see just how wrong I was to extend this olive branch.

Still, it hurts all the same. These are my parents—my only family and they have washed their hands of me. That is, unless I cease this devil-worship at once and stop my unholy communications, I shall never hear from him or my mother again. They are both disgusted with my chosen path and do not believe I could be their offspring. The notion they would attend my graduation from such a heinous institution is insulting.

As such, I am never to write them again.

Tears stream down my cheeks, catching on the parchment as it flutters onto my desk. I should burn it—pay a hexes student to cast one upon him for his cruelty, but I can't bring myself to. All I feel is achingly alone. I should call for Prue, but she's happy with Zander.

She would understand, but I don't wish to put this burden on her, especially when her love is so new. She is a good friend to me—always taking me home with her during the holidays and never asking why. Her parents are just as kind, including me in their traditions in ways my parents never would. I am grateful to have them.

Still, I wish I had someone like she has Zander. If I could

turn to another for comfort, my family's final disownment would sting less. I wouldn't have to explain myself; they could just hold me and let the tears flow for the family I'll never have.

Besides, it's my fault for inviting them in the first place. My loneliness had gotten the better of me all those weeks ago and encouraged me to write it. I'd take it back if I could—as I would all those awful memories.

Suddenly, my room is too hot, and the scent of lilacs overwhelms my senses. I rush to the window and throw it open, allowing a cold breeze to disturb the contents of my room. Tearing at my clothes, I shed them as quickly as I can. Once naked, I see my pale skin marred with red along my chest and knees—a fine sheen of sweat dots my forehead.

Turning slightly, I stare at them in the light from my candles—a permanent reminder of their hatred for what I truly am. My fingers graze over the raised and puckered skin. I remember receiving each one and being told that a parent's love is not given—it is earned—and I will surely never earn theirs.

A sob catches in my throat. Exhaustion flows through me. I wish Bael were here.

The thought appears so suddenly, and yet I cannot deny it. My heart reaches for him—calls to him on the wind as if there was any way he could hear me. I know his being here would make me feel better. He would make me whole again if his feelings for me were genuine. He would allow me to cry in his arms and soothe me through it, continuously reminding me that I wasn't alone.

That loving me wasn't something I had to earn.

A fresh wave of sadness spreads throughout my body. I am alone tonight. I should take a sip of my sleeping dram before the nightmares appear tonight. However, I can't bring myself to do anything except slide on a silk nightgown, crawl into bed, and curl up under the quilt.

The candles in my room go out in an instant. In the dark, I let myself sob and sob until exhaustion makes me delirious. Before I succumb to the darkness, something flutters at my window. A raven has returned, but I swear, just before I'm pulled into sleep, I glimpse its eyes.

Ones that are the same shade as Bael's.

15

THE HIGH WARLOCK

He should've stayed a bird and remained perched on her window.

Venturing into her room was a gross misstep, but he couldn't help himself. He had to come and see her. He had felt her reach for him—call out to him in a way only his kind can fully understand. Still, he should've remained distant and never looked through her things.

Seeing her tear-stained cheeks and hearing her soft whimpers snapped something inside of him. What was the cause of her distress? What had brought such sadness to someone so vibrant?

When he had spied the letter on her desk, everything became clear. A hot rush of anger swam in his blood—the desire to find the one responsible and tear him apart was palpable. How could anyone send someone as lovely as Darcee such vile words?

He wanted to demand answers from her and make those responsible pay, but as her breathing finally turned deep and even, he decided to remain a silent visitor. Her room was exactly as he remembered from watching her days ago. Being inside of it was even better than he imagined.

Everything smelt like Darcee—the fresh scent of his lilac bouquet mixed with her unique smell. Everything was pink, from her bedding to the frilly clothes spilling out of her closet. Used candles and incense littered her desk. Various spell jars and an empty cauldron sat near her altar. He thumbed through a book entitled *My Lovers*, expecting to find a list of all the people Darcee had been with.

Not that he much cared; the past was the past, but he was curious—wanting to know everything about her, even in an unethical way. However, it wasn't a list of her lovers but all those she had brought together. As he went through each page, pride swam in his chest.

She was a talented love witch, of that he was sure. Her kindness and compassion danced through every story. No wonder he had always been drawn to her—Darcee is frightfully easy to love.

He would know.

His eyes find the note again. Reading it over again, his anger burns hot. How could a father write this to his daughter? His hands began to tremble. If only he knew—

"Bael?" Darcee's soft voice cuts through the room.

He turns on his heel, knowing that a quick transformation is out of the question. She's spotted him, and he should own up to it now.

Her eyes are wide, and her hair is a mess of pink curls. She holds a thin pink sheet to her chest as if it or the scrap of fabric she calls a nightgown conceals any part of her. Swaths of pale skin are on display, glimmering in the moonlight. Her lips are still puffy from his kisses earlier.

His entire body hardens in an instant at the delicious sight of her.

Darcee's magenta eyes blink under lowered brows.

"Bael?" she repeats. "Is—is that you?"

The apprehension in her voice spurns him to wave his hand. Her candles blaze to life and illuminate the dark room. She blinks again to adjust to the light. If she was a vision in moonlight, candlelight makes her a divine goddess.

"It's me," he says, taking a small step towards her.

She sags with relief, falling back against the mountain of pillows stuffed behind her. Her bed is a mess of pink satin sheets and a ruffled quilt hanging entirely off one side.

"I didn't mean to frighten you." His voice is gentler than he's ever heard it.

"How did you get in here?"

Reluctantly, he nods towards the open window.

"Flew in."

"I knew that bird had your eyes," she mumbles, a yawn sneaking up.

He nods, not knowing what else to say. Darcee's eyes soften as she stares at him.

"Why did you come?"

He licks his lips—she deserves the truth—all of it. For now, he'll settle for giving her only some.

"I heard you call to me."

Her eyes widened.

"You—you did?" She shakes her head. "I didn't even know what I was doing—only knew that I wanted you here. With me."

"And here I am. When I discovered you were sad, I couldn't—I wouldn't..." He swallows loudly, coming to stand at the foot of her bed. "Will you tell me why you were crying?"

Darcee's lovely face pales to an alarming degree. With a quick shake of her head, the misery in her eyes nearly makes his knees buckle.

"It's a long, terrible story."

A tenderness he's only felt towards Darcee hums in his veins. A moment of silence stretches as they watch each other.

"I should go. It was wrong for me to enter your room without you knowing."

Turning from her bed, he makes his way back over to the window. Metal coats his tongue as he prepares to transform into his avian form. His fingers flex, but before he can release the spell, Darcee calls to him.

"Wait," she says, eyes dancing around the room. "I wanted you to come here tonight—to be with me."

Reaching out a delicate hand, the sheet falls to her waist. The nightgown barely conceals her breasts, yet his attention is only on her face. There is a vulnerability there he's never seen before. That letter has left her rattled. She called him because she needed him here when she was feeling vulnerable.

"Stay with me."

He follows it like the command that it is. He removes his shoes and shirt until he is in nothing but a pair of silk trousers. He takes her extended hand and kisses the back of her palm, delighting in her shiver. He pulls back the sheets and quilt and settles in beside her.

They both say nothing as he curls around her, dragging her back until her spine is flush with his chest. His arm slides under her pillow, and the other drapes along her waist. They fit together perfectly as if they were made for each other.

He inhales her scent and lets it soothe him. Darcee sighs contently in his arms.

"You're so warm." The words are barely a whisper.

Her breathing turns deep and even. Tonight wasn't about desire or passion. No, it was about something more important: comfort. She called for him and no one else. She wanted him.

Good, he thinks. *She is mine. Now and forever.*

He counts her breaths until sleep claims him, too.

16

DARCEE

As soon as I open my eyes, I remember I'm not alone. Golden sunlight pours into my room, and the soft singing of birds filters through the open window. In the morning light, I can see the piles of dirty clothes littering the floor, the haphazard stacks of books, and dried herbs that desperately need to be put away. Everything is exactly the same.

All except the very warm male body lying against my side.

His warm hand digs softly into my hip. The soft tendrils of his hair tickle my naked shoulder. The muscles of his chest rise and fall behind me. I had expected him to slip out sometime during the night, but finding him still here this morning is a delight.

My slumber had been deep and dreamless. It was restorative in a way I haven't experienced in a long time, especially with the lack of sleeping aid. With Bael spooned around me, the sting of my father's dismissal has lessened considerably. I can put it far from my mind and enjoy being wrapped in another's arms.

I inhale deeply, shifting slightly backward. Bael's hard cock presses against my backside. My mouth goes dry at his impressive length. I do it again, failing to stop the moan slipping from my lips. Bael inhales sharply from behind me, coming fully awake. With a deep groan, I feel his lips move at my ear.

"Good morning," he murmurs.

I swallow. "Morning."

It feels natural waking up with him like this—as if we have done it a million times before. Bael's large hand tightens on my waist, gently skimming up and down. The thin fabric of my nightgown is barely a barrier. His hands may as well be on my naked flesh.

"I planned only to stay until you fell asleep," he admits quietly. "You just felt so good, I couldn't bring myself to leave."

I hear the smile in his voice.

"Besides," he continues, "waking up next to you has its advantages."

"Oh?" I ask, turning my head to look at him. "Like what?"

His deep chuckle sets my blood on fire. Desire—hot and heavy—runs through me. The arm resting under my head moves slowly as it creeps under my body and towards my front. It splays along my ribs before tracing maddening circles on the underside of my breast. The hand on my waist moves, too, shifting lower before gliding under the hem of my nightgown.

"Is this okay?" he asks.

The first brush of his fingers against my hard nipple causes my whole body to go taught.

"Yes," I sigh, eyes fluttering closed. "More."

His hand wraps around the thin strap of my nightgown and tugs it down. I gasp as my breast is exposed to the cool morning air. Bael snarls against me. His hand cups my breast, squeezing it gently. I peel my eyes open to take in the sight.

Gray skin compliments my own—pink and with a dusting of freckles. My breast sits perfectly in the palm of his hands. Like our kiss yesterday, his movements aren't practiced. When his thumb drags over my nipple, I moan, and that seems to guide him. His fingers work me, teasing and playing with me until my breath is uneven.

Wetness pools between my thighs, and I rub them together for any sort of relief. The hand resting on my hip inches higher, but slowly as if unsure.

"Darcee," he whispers in my ear. "Tell me what you want—I've never—"

My eyes bore into him as a heady rush flows through me. Right now, there is only us in this room. How we got here is not important. At least, that's what I tell myself. How can something this right come from something so wrong?

I push it all from my mind—the love potion, the former mutual disdain—and absorb what Bael offers me. We will not take it too far. I will allow him to touch me because he wishes to, and as awful as I am to admit it, if I stop this now, I feel as though I may die from longing.

My hand comes up and cups his atop my breast.

"Like this," I say softly. "Touch me like this."

Together, we work in tandem as he begins squeezing and molding my breasts in his hand. Reaching down, I find his other hand on my waist. I crane my head back and meet his lips with mine. His eyes flare before closing. Bael tastes of spice and midnight air. Our lips meet—slow at first—and then quicken with intensity. I could spend hours at a time kissing him. For what he lacks in experience, he makes up for in enthusiasm.

My hand digs into his as I slowly drag it to my front. Once again, sensation moves me as I settle his palm against the wet heat of my most intimate flesh. Bael hisses into my mouth as he cups me. My whimper echoes between us.

"Touch me here."

His hand squeezes me again, and my breathing turns ragged.

"Darcee."

The growl of my name is the only warning I get before my

body leaves the mattress. Bael rises into a sitting position and gathers me to his front—my spine molds to his chest. In the morning light, everything is visible. There is no sheet to hide what we are doing. Over my shoulder, his mouth finds mine. I gasp against him when I feel him tug the other strap of my nightgown down.

The fabric pools as my waist, leaving me naked from the chest up. I'm glad for this position—it conceals the markings on my back—I don't want those awful memories to ruin this beautiful morning. Bael's hand alternates between my nipples, working them as his tongue tangles with mine.

My legs spread of their own accord, propping themselves up so that he has better access to me. The sunlight reveals the messy state of my sheets below us. A breeze blows in from the open window, washing us in the scent of fresh grass. All I smell is Bael. All I taste is him. He is everywhere—embedded in the very fibers of my soul.

He breaks our kiss to stare down at me. My skin is flushed, and sweat pools at my temples. His heavy breaths move along my back, and I can feel the pounding of his heart. It matches the rhythm of my own.

"Beautiful," he growls, tracing a finger through my wetness, and my head lolls against his shoulder. "Mine."

His declaration should scare me—it should wake me from whatever sexual haze I'm in and end this. It's already gone too far, and I can't stop it. I can't do anything but thrust myself against his soft touch. I am conflicted over all of this, but there is no denying how much I want him. It isn't because I want to play along for the potion. It's because he's Bael.

The male who came when I called him, who held me through the night and offered me comfort, who understood everything without asking a single question, who made me feel like, for the first time in my life, I wasn't alone.

Is it wrong to enjoy this now, knowing soon he will return to hating me? I don't have an answer to that. All I know is that right now, it's just us. My morals have already been compromised. I might as well go all in with it now.

His long finger skims through my wetness again, brushing my clit as he goes. A gasp rasps out of me, the pleasure already intense.

"There," I sigh, turning back to look at him. "More."

Bael's eyes darken as he applies brush to that little bundle of nerves. His fingers are too firm at first, but I quickly remedy that with a kiss and a command of *softer*. It's not long before he finds his rhythm. Together, he works my pussy and nipples, heightening my pleasure to levels I didn't know were possible.

I'm never this easy to please. Typically, it takes a lot more work and longer for me even to feel close to climaxing. As it stands, Bael only needs to sink a finger inside of me, and I'll be on the precipice of my peak.

"Bael."

His hand makes deliciously sloppy sounds as he works me. My hips move of their own accord, grinding against his circling fingers. My arm curls around his shoulders, and he lifts me further up his chest. More of me is exposed to his greedy eyes. Bending down, he presses a kiss to the side of my breasts.

"Darcee—tell me what you need. How can I—"

"Inside," I gasp. "Put your fingers inside me."

Bael growls like a beast. Tightening his grip on my breast one last time, he lowers it to my hip. His other hand skims lower, coating his fingers in my wetness. His finger traces around my entrance, and my legs inch further apart. The muscles of my thighs begin to burn, but it pales in comparison to the fire raging inside me.

He tucks a finger just into my opening, and my head falls back. The only thing keeping me upright is his other hand holding firm. Slowly, he sinks the whole finger inside of me. He wiggles it around, retreating partially and then plunging it back inside. My stucco moans encourage him to do it again—faster, harder.

It's not long before he adds a second one and stretches me. He pumps them quickly, curling in a way that brushes a secret spot inside me that blurs my vision. Bael brings his other hand to work my clit, and I'm done for.

"Bael—oh Goddess, I'm close." The words spill from my lips.

His fingers continue to fuck me—tunneling in and out over and over. The pressure on my clit is perfect. My peak looms ahead, tantalizingly close.

"I need to feel it, Darcee. Reward me with your pleasure. Soak my hand with your sweet come." His lips curl against my head. "Then I'll lick your little pussy clean."

I've never heard Bael use foul language before. Those crude words race through my body and send me tumbling over the edge. I scream out his name—metal dances in the air as all the candles on my desk blaze to life. My magic and pleasure have never been tied before, but with Bael, anything seems possible.

Fire licks at my skin, and my tight muscles eventually relax. Bael never stops working me. The wet sounds of his fingers pumping me only intensify as I do indeed soak his hand. Once I am spent, and my body is trembling against him, I watch through heavy-lidded eyes as he sucks my come from each finger.

The grin he gives me is wicked, and my body is already heating up for more.

"Delicious, little witch. I need more."

He slides out from behind me, and my head falls to the mountain of pillows against my headboard. Crawling between my spread thighs, he looks almost comically large, stuffed at the end of my small bed. His smile is pure male satisfaction as he stares down at me. I don't feel shy—quite the opposite as my legs inch even farther apart.

Bael smirks. "Naughty."

I bat my eyelashes at him. "Who me?"

"Yes, you."

His warm lips kiss the inside of my left knee while his hand skims up and down my other thigh. Inhaling deeply, his eyes focus on my sensitive flesh. Again, I watch his lips twist.

"I knew it."

I arch a brow. "Knew what?"

Lowering his head to my center, he tosses my legs over his shoulder. Cupping my bottom, he brings me towards his face, lifting my lower half entirely off the bed. His tongue licks over his bottom lip.

"That you'd be perfectly pink here as well."

I moan at the first press of his tongue. Bael is a quick learner because he devours me without any aid. Normally, I have to be vocal during this part—I've rarely found a man who knows exactly what I want, but Bael understands. His tongue is firm in its exploration. Those plush lips I'll dream about kissing until I die, suck at my clit, and cause my thighs to tremble.

Whether it's because I'm already on edge from my previous orgasm or because it's Bael, I don't know, but my climax is already looming. His fingers dig into the globes of my ass, holding me fast to his face. I grind myself against his tongue, urging him to spear it into me.

Once he does and tastes me whole, I am awash in flame. I choke out his name as my thighs clamp around his head. He holds me through it, sucking and licking as I finally come down. With one final lick to my pussy, he lowers my hips back to the bed. Bael's violet eyes glow anew as he kisses my stomach and then higher.

He licks his way back up my body before our mouths meet again. I can taste myself on his tongue, and I shiver in response. Propping himself up on his elbows, I can still feel his hardness digging into my stomach. My hands skim down his chest before reaching for the bulge in his pants.

Just as he did before, his hand wraps around my wrist, stopping me.

"Before we do that, little witch, there's something I have to explain first." He takes a deep breath. "Look, I'm—"

A loud bang at my door interrupts him.

"Darcee! Are you up? We have class in ten minutes." There is another series of bangs before the doorknob begins to jiggle. "Why is your door locked?"

"Fuck!" I push at Bael's chest to let me up. He reluctantly slides to the side as I tug my nightgown back into place. "Be right there, Prue!"

I pull on a pair of panties and rush to my closet. Tossing a soft pink sweater over my head, I pull my nightgown off underneath it and throw it somewhere on the floor. Finding a black pleated skirt, I quickly zip it on before hunting down socks and my favorite white boots. Once I am dressed, I turn towards the bed.

Bael is lounging on his side, a smile playing on his face. In the morning light, I can see just how muscular he is. He is not bulky but lean with a clear definition. My mouth waters at the sight, and I wonder if skipping my charms class is worth it.

Another bang quickly eradicates that idea.

"Darcee! Unlock the door, let's go!"

Bael chuckles and slides off my bed. Prowling towards me, I stare up at him transfixed. His hand tucks a loose curl behind my ear.

"I'll slip out the window before you open the door, but I wanted to give you this. My courtship is still in effect even after our delicious detour."

I grin up at him, a fresh blush warming my cheeks. With a wave of his hand, he pulls a small box seemingly out of nowhere from behind my ear.

"Parlor magic? Aren't you a little old for such tricks?"

"Never."

He grins and opens the top of the small velvet box. A dainty silver chain with a large rose quartz shaped like a heart rests on a tiny pillow. My breath catches, and I meet his gaze.

"Bael, I—"

"Since you've stolen my heart, I thought you should wear it too."

He looks so damn sincere I feel tears pooling in my eyes.

"That was so ridiculously cheesy. And this is far too much."

"For you, it's not nearly enough." His lips press against mine. "Will you wear it?"

I nod, blinking the wetness from my eyes. "Of course."

He quickly secures the dainty chain around my neck. The stone falls against my chest, and I feel it hum with power. Another barrage of banging comes from the door as Prue laments that we are about to be late.

Bael kisses me again. It's over far too quickly. Without another word, he seamlessly transforms into a raven and flies out the open window. I watch him go momentarily before rushing to collect my cloak and belongings.

Unlocking the door, I push out into the hall. Prue's blue eyes narrow on me as I greet her with a genuinely frazzled grin.

"Sorry, I overslept. My alarm didn't go off."

"Right." Prue doesn't sound overly convinced. Her eyes linger on my chest for a moment. "Is that necklace new?"

We turn and make our way down the hall. My hand goes to the stone; it pulses against my palm like a real heart. Glancing up at her, I nod.

"Yes, I got it, um—"

Prue chuckles and shakes her head.

"No need to lie, Dar. I'm all ears when you want to tell me about the mystery man I heard you talking to in your room."

I choke on a breath, and that only deepens Prue's grin.

"You've always been a dreadful liar. Is it someone I know?." She tosses her arm around my shoulder as the bell rings overhead, signaling that we are, in fact, very late.

Goddess, how badly I want to come clean and admit it all to her. She would give me advice on what to do, advice that I probably wouldn't want to hear since it would mean recognizing that the most fantastic pleasure was wrong and that it could never happen again.

Therefore, because I am an awful, unethical witch, my confession never comes. I merely smile at my friend and give a slight nod.

"It's someone you know very well."

Prue giggles as the two of us continue down the desolate hall. My hand tugs tighter on the stone, letting the rhythmic pounding soothe me.

I may have stolen his heart because of a love potion, but it's abundantly clear I've carelessly given mine away to him. I don't think I'll get it back in one piece when all this is over.

17

DARCEE

The day passes in a blur.

Every time my thighs rub together, I remember what Bael felt like between them: his warm breath, the scent of skin, and the feel of his silken hair on my bare skin. My mind had been wandering all day, replaying the wonderful morning and knowing it should never happen again.

I know that, and yet, as I sit next to Prue at our workbench and watch Bael flit around the room explaining the properties of a plant I've never heard of, I'm desperate to feel his touch again. I'm powerless when it comes to my desire—and I've never wanted anyone as badly as him. It's not unheard of for me to fall for someone too quickly—I am a love witch.

Usually, what ends up happening is I realize I'm more in love with the idea of them—their potential—than who they are. Bael is the opposite of that. The way he presented himself to me initially put me off. After seeing the softer, more compassionate side, I'm rapidly falling for the male I've discovered.

The one who cares for me in a way I've always dreamed of. While I love his gifts, I adore the compassion he's shown me. From helping with my grade to holding me last night and keeping the nightmares away, it's no wonder I'm in danger of losing my heart to him.

Especially when I've opened my textbooks throughout the day to find little love notes tucked between the pages, each one was some abysmal riddle that made my heart pound and skin tingle. They are adorable, and I'll cherish every single one of them forever.

I wonder—not for the first time—if we could have had this without the love potion. Would this relationship have formed naturally if I had come to him for help organically? It just seems so easy. For all I know about love potions, I am truly out of my depth with this one. It has shown no signs of waning, though our little tryst this morning surely didn't help the situation.

Again, I vow that if it hasn't completely gotten out of his system by graduation, I will take matters into my own hands. I was leaving that night anyway. The first day of my lease starts the day of graduation. I needed to be open immediately if I had any hope of making the next month's rent.

I can make it through one more week of this. The end of our relationship—if it can even be called that—is a matter of when, not if.

Deep in thought, I barely register the bell ringing until those around me pack up to leave and shuffle out the door. Prue is already on her feet, stuffing her books into her bag and looking at me expectantly.

"Zander and I are going to research bog creatures at the cafe if you want to come. I know nothing about that place, and we're going in a couple of days."

I glance over to Bael leaning against the front of his desk. Formidable and grumpy, yet he had eaten my pussy like he was starving, and I was the feast he'd waited his whole life for. It's a delicious secret that our surly professor burns hotly for me. The gleam in his eyes tells me he knows what I'm thinking. Heat swims in my cheeks as I turn back towards my friend.

"I—I—um can't. Professor Fangborne is giving me extra lessons after class to help raise my grade before graduation." Prue lowers her brows. "Did—I, um, not mention that yesterday?"

"No," she says. "You've been acting strange. Is everything okay?"

The truth is on the tip of my tongue, but I swallow it back down.

"Everything is fine, Prue. I've just been forgetful lately. Graduation brain, you know?"

My best friend purses her lips.

"You've been forgetting a lot lately. Like the fact that I can read auras and yours, my sweet friend, is pinker than usual."

My mouth goes dry.

"I'm sure I don't know what you're talking about," I say, waving a dismissive hand.

Her dark brows lower, but Zander appears before she can push me on it. He nods at me before taking my friend's hand.

"This conversation isn't over, Dar."

"See you later," I say, waving at them as Zander pulls her down the hall.

As much as I long to confess to her, I don't want to put her in that position. If the school found out she knew and didn't report it, she could also be in serious trouble. I'll keep it to myself for now. How have I made such a mess in only a few days?

Once the final student exits, I hear the door to the room bolt shut. Bael remains in front of his desk, eyeing me carefully. I rise on shaking knees and collect my belongings. His hungry gaze devours me whole the closer I get. I'd love nothing more for him to toss me over his desk and give me a repeat of this morning, but we have work to do.

He grins down at me, his hand falling to the small of my back as he guides me towards his office.

"Let's see how much you've retrained from yesterday."

Inside his office, the purple fire is barely flickering. Atop his desk are a variety of herbs and a bubbling cauldron. Inside a delicate white teacup is a dark-colored liquid. The scent is putrid, and the steam rising over the lip of the cup looks like smoke.

"Nightshade tea," he explains from beside me. "Extremely deadly. Your task is to make it safe to drink based on the properties we discussed in our last session."

I glance up at him. Surely, he is joking. His eyes, however, are earnest. The hand on my back falls away as he leans down closer. Finding my ear, his words are a whispered promise.

"If you do good, I'll reward you once our lesson is done."

A sigh escapes me, and I nearly collapse to the floor. Instantly, he pulls away with a grin on his lips and retreats to the other side of the desk. I drop my things to the floor and survey the ingredients before me.

"Okay," I say, grabbing a fresh sprig of rosemary. "Here goes nothing."

An hour later, my eyes feel like they're filled with sand.

My head pounds and my magic is officially spent for the rest of the day. As I stare down at the teacup, which no longer seems ominously dark, I can only hope I counteracted enough of its properties to make it drinkable. Bael oversaw me the whole time, gently nudging me in the right direction but ultimately leaving this first test up to me.

I sink into my chair, exhaustion weighing me down.

"Finished?" Bael asks, reaching for the mug.

Nodding, I can no longer even form words.

Bael gives it a tentative sniff. Apprehension tickles the back of my neck. I did all that I could, but I still wouldn't drink it. He doesn't plan to—

Before I can say anything, Bael puts his lips on the cup and consumes one large swallow. If I haven't broken down the poison enough, that sip means death in a few minutes. My mouth falls open, and I lean forward in my chair. Bael's body tenses as he swallows. After a few moments pass, he appears no worse for wear—and he's breathing, which is a very positive sign.

Violet eyes meet mine and I'm happy to see them clear.

"Not bad," he says softly.

Pride floods my veins. I did it?

"Really?" I ask, reaching for the cup.

Bael snatches it from me before I can bring it to my lips. Walking on his long legs towards the fireplace, he quickly tosses it into the low-burning fire. It hisses, and an eruption of black smoke billows from the hearth. Bael returns to me and sets the cup down.

"Not bad, but still poisonous."

I deflate like a balloon falling back into my chair. I'm truly hopeless at this.

"You forgot one key ingredient," he says, nodding towards the end of the table.

My eyes land on the glass pot of licorice root. Goddess, I had forgotten all about that. It was the exact thing I needed to counteract the final properties. Without it, the poison was still deadly.

"I knew I was forgetting something," I mumble before my whole body freezes. "Wait, how come you aren't dead?"

Bael chuckles, waving a dismissive hand.

"My kind are immune to such things."

"That's handy." I cross my arms over my chest and lean

forward. "So what are you exactly? That is if you don't mind telling me."

Bael smiles softly.

"I'll tell you whatever you want to know, Darcee."

I blush in delight.

"My father was a demon from beyond the veil. On the winter solstice, my mother had summoned him, and well—one thing led to another, and I was born. As a halfling, I have some of my father's power, and I can see into the veil more easily than others. As you've seen, I also have some of his more beastly attributes. And his long lifespan."

"Is he still around? Do you see him?"

Bael's lips turn down. Sadness dances over his features.

"No, my mother and he passed away a few decades ago."

My hand comes down on his, and I thread our fingers together before squeezing him.

"I'm sorry for your loss, Bael."

He smiles at me before gently tugging on my hand. I rise and round his desk, as he pushes back into his chair. I allow him to settle me into his lap, feeling whole again for the first time since this morning. His hands go to my waist, gently squeezing me.

"While it wasn't perfect, this attempt was much better than your last."

"No explosion this time, you mean? I ruined my favorite sweater that day."

We share a smile, clearly remembering the screaming students and the walls painted in a thick goo. I had just thrown everything into the cauldron and hoped for the best. Now I see how foolish that had been.

"In any case, a reward for improvement is undoubtedly in order."

I giggle as he rises with me in his arms. With a wave of his hand, his desk is wiped clear of our lesson, and he settles me on the smooth surface. The cool wood seeps into my clothes and soothes my heated skin. There's something decadent about letting him have me in here. His large frame looms over me before he sinks to his knees.

His face is at the perfect height of my heated core. I prop up on my elbows and lift my hips as he reaches beneath my skirt and slips off my satin panties. I watch him tuck them into his pocket as his hands slide up my booted legs and hook me around the waist. He drags me closer to the edge and flips up my skirt, baring me fully to his hungry gaze.

"I think Prue knows about us," I blurt out.

It may be my half-hearted attempt to stop this before it begins. One touch from him and all my protests will be silenced. Bael's eyes bore into mine, his mouth inches away from where I need him.

"Does the idea bother you?" he asks.

Licking my lips, I avoid the question.

"I don't like lying to my friend."

"Once you graduate, we no longer have to hide." His fingers dance up and down my thighs. "I would publicly claim you, but I understand how it could look to some."

"We should be more discreet." My protest is half-hearted at best. "Maybe we should take a step back and—"

The broad side of Bael's tongue licks up my pussy and cuts me off. My body heats at the slight touch. His hands on my hips tighten, and he stares up at me.

"Do you want me to stop, little witch?"

He swipes at my flesh with his tongue again, and my mouth falls open.

"Darcee," he prompts against my wet flesh.

"N—no."

His smile is pure satisfaction.

"Good girl."

Without wasting another moment, he devours me like he

did this morning. His tongue laps at me before sucking my clit into his mouth. He loves it with his tongue, kissing it gently before nuzzling it with his nose. He inhales fully as if savoring the scent of my arousal. The wet glide of his tongue pushes into my entrance, and I grind my hips against his face.

The silken glide of his hair against my inner thighs sets my blood on fire: my heart pounds, and my head races. The scent of our coupling mixes with his earthy smell. It overwhelms me and pools in my lungs. Wet sounds echo from between my legs as he continues to feast.

His hand slips from my hips. Bael sucks his fingers into his mouth, wetting them before he spears them gently into my heated center. He pumps them just as he did before, curling them expertly. Moans and sighs pour from between my lips as my peak looms closer. Bael lashes at my clit with his tongue as his fingers work me.

I feel a third one begin to stretch me, and my muscles snap tight. There is nothing but pleasure. I am awash in the scent and feel of Bael. There is only us. Nothing else exists beyond my pleasure. I scream his name. My legs lock around his face as my body comes clean off the desk.

He licks me through my orgasm, prolonging it until I am a quivering mess atop his desk. My eyes can barely focus. I feel him rise to his feet rather than see it. Leaning down, he scoops me into his arms and settles me against his chest again. His lips find mine, sharing my taste and lazily exploring my mouth. The cool leather arms of the chair bracket my thighs.

"You are my madness, too," I confess.

His eyes flash, and he kisses me harder. My soul reaches for his, but I stop it from completely unfurling—it's the last shred of myself I haven't wholly relinquished to him.

The growing length of his cock presses into me, and I shift against it. Breaking our kiss, I stare into his violet eyes.

"Why do you never ask me to pleasure you?"

Licking his lips, his hands drift up my back to shift through my curls. He sighs, leaning back against the chair.

"My kind has different rules when it comes to...physical intimacy."

Apprehension seeps into my stomach.

"Go on."

Bael's smile is small as he curls a lock of my hair around his finger.

"We mate for life," he says simply. "Before we find the one we want to spend the rest of our lives with, we do not engage in any sort of release."

My tongue sticks to the roof of my mouth at his confession. Bael is a virgin. His inexperience now makes a lot more sense. With him being older, I assumed he was just out of practice or maybe was used to being with his kind. Now, it's all adding up.

"Oh, Goddess, have I—have we crossed a line? Did you not want me to—"

Bael silences me with a kiss.

"I would gladly take you back to my cottage and make love to you all night. Never doubt the depth of my devotion to you. It's why I wanted to court you properly—to make sure you are certain. If you allow me to claim you, our lives will become one." His smile is breathtaking. "If you require more time, I will gladly wait. And if you are never ready, that is okay too."

"But you want me?"

"More than I've ever wanted anything in my life."

His hand cups my cheek.

And there it is, the clear line in the sand. The line I will never cross. Taking that next step with him could never be undone. I'm glad he stopped me all those times I reached to pleasure him. If we had taken it too far, and he had bound himself to me only to wake from the potion's stupor and realize what he'd done, I'd never forgive myself.

No, that is one thing I cannot take from him. While I'd love to give myself to him and live our lives together, I cannot. I should slide off his lap and tell him this was all a mistake. I'll take my failing grade and find some way not to have to repeat the class and delay my graduation hopes. Or better yet, I should confess to what I've done, give him an antidote, and accept the consequences.

Yet, I look at the hope in his eyes, I know doing either of those things would crush him right now. As much as it sickens me to do so, I know what I have to say. How much worse can another lie make things?

"After graduation," I say.

Bael lowers his brows, and I press a kiss to it.

"After graduation—when we no longer have to hide and you're no longer my teacher—we will—I will—become yours."

His smile is beautiful enough to break my heart.

"It's perfect," he says. "You, Darcee, are so perfect."

I blush, my giggle all too real.

"It can be your graduation present to me."

He helps me to my feet and collects my belongings as we enter the main room. The door to the room unlocks, and the sound triggers a memory.

"What did Romina want yesterday?"

Bael shrugs. "For me to sign off on a few teaching aids. Why do you ask?"

"No reason," I say. "You know she likes you, right? Surely, you've noticed. She's all the subtlety of an angered snake."

The High Warlock chokes on a laugh.

"I hardly notice anything about Romina. I only have eyes for you."

My lips pull up at the side.

"Good answer," I say, pulling him down for one last parting kiss.

His hand lands on my backside and pulls me deeper into him. I moan in surprise, letting our tongues tangle. We savor each other as the evening bell chimes. Reluctantly, we pull apart. His thumb traces my swollen lips.

"Possessive little thing you are."

I am when I have no right to be.

"Are you coming to my room tonight?" I ask.

I should tell him not to, but I'm not that strong.

"If you'd like me to. I promise to be on my best behavior."

Shaking my head, I smile as I walk towards the door.

"I'll leave the window open."

18

DARCEE

My heavy pack only adds to my uncomfortability. The evening sun is low, casting heavy shadows on me and all the other necromancy students gathered in the courtyard. The weekend has come, and it is time to venture into *the Bog*. Prue stands beside me, her pack laden with various supplies to gather what we're looking for.

Outside, I note for the first time how small our class is. Amongst the whispering students is Bael, a piece of parchment in hand, as he checks us each off for attendance. His eyes dance over me, a secretive smile on his lips, before he moves on to check the next student.

We've spent every night together this past week. He comes to me as a raven, flying in after I'm already in bed and wrapping me in his arms. The nightmares are gone when he is with me— sleep is either dreamless or of him.

We keep things tame in the mornings, cuddling close in the early dawn hours. That is where we share stories of ourselves. Bael tells me of his loving childhood—of growing up different but always the center of his parents' world. I keep my past vague enough, and he doesn't pry. I tell him stories of Prue and all the happy couples I've brought together. He praises my skill.

When it is time to get up, he leaves me with a chaste kiss. One I feel until I see him later for our tutoring session. Prue hasn't questioned me about them or her opinions of my very pink aura. I know she has questions for me, and I can't avoid them forever.

Bael's and I's connection has only grown stronger. The potion has shown no signs of lessening. I expect him to wake up alarmed each night in my bed, demanding to know what he's doing in there. Or for him to grow irritated at me during tutoring and grace me with a disdainful glower. Neither happens.

In fact, after a week of lessons, I retook my first and second exams and received a passing grade. We will finish the last one before the final grades are submitted. No matter how I perform on my final exam, I'll graduate on time if all goes well with this last test.

Bael has been pleased with my improvements. If our nights and mornings together are chaste, the tutoring sessions are where we indulge. He is steadfast in his promise to keep things professional while teaching me. Yet, after both tests, he rewarded me with his mouth on my aching flesh. I've lost count of the times he's made me come over the past week.

I long to feel his cock buried inside of me—for our connection to grow more profound—but then I remember why I can't let it.

We've shared so much with each other. He told me of his travels before becoming a professor. I've told him of my desire to become a professional love witch and open my own shop. Each day that passes, I sink deeper into him.

I'll miss him terribly when this is over. I don't know if I'll ever sleep peacefully without his arms around me.

Bael clears his throat, and everyone's attention snaps towards him.

"Students, for your final exam, you will need to travel into *the Bog*."

I try not to physically recoil at the idea. I hate *the Bog*. The smell, the nightmarish creatures who call it home, the overgrown trees, and the swampy grounds that will leave my bare legs caked in mud. It will be a trek to get there, and this pack is already causing my back to ache.

Bael adjusts the small bag on his shoulder, looking completely unruffled and handsome.

"It is there you will find the *evernight mushroom*. Its properties will be needed to complete your reanimation brews next week."

Before, the thought of tampering with a corpse made my stomach roll. Now, I've come to understand the beauty in such things. There is balance in all magic, and while necromancy and I will always be the opposite, I have a newfound appreciation for it, thanks to Bael.

"It is up to you to locate and retrieve the fungus properly. We will camp on my property, where my wards protect you. The *evernight mushroom* will glow at dusk and only be visible for a few hours. Work fast to retrieve it, and don't lose your way in *the Bog*."

Turning from the group, Bael leads them forward. A few eager students race towards the front, engaging Bael in animated conversation. He nods thoughtfully, offering up one-word responses. I can't help but laugh.

My high ponytail does nothing to help the sweat on my brow. I had to purchase new clothes just for this hike. None came in pink, so I'm dressed in olive green shorts and a fitted white top that's supposed to be breathable. My feet are laced into sturdy brown boots I will never wear again.

Slowing my pace, I linger at the back of the group. As if he senses me drifting away, Bael glances back to ensure I am okay. I give him a slight nod and resume walking forward. My heart squeezes in my chest. To have this secret affection between us is a thrill—if only it were real.

Bael constantly talks about his excitement for graduation. He can't wait for us to stop sneaking around and for me to finally be his. This will be our last week together, and while part of me wants to savor these final moments, it may be time to start pulling back, even if the thought abhors me.

Next week, I'll make the antidote and give it enough time to charge before graduation. I'll find a way to slip it to him after the ceremony.

The terrain around us darkens as we enter the *Wicked Woods*. Gnarled branches interlock overhead. Ancient roots burst through the ground like fingers, snagging at our ankles. I nearly lose my footing several times but manage to stay upright. My eyes are trained on Bael. His tall frame parts through the thick thatch of trees until we are on a smoother path.

His graceful gait is entrancing. I watch his large hands come up and hold up a branch for the student behind him to pass under. I know just what those hands feel like on my skin. How tender they can be as they hold me while I sleep. Not to mention the intense pleasure they can bring when slipping inside—

"Your aura is so pink I can hardly see you," Prue whispers at my side.

I gasp and lose my footing on the slippery ground. Her hand cups my elbow, steadying me. Her blue eyes are serious as we stand face to face. The group quickly files around us to pass under the low-hanging tree.

Prue crosses her arms over her chest, the straps of her pack digging into her shoulders.

"What's going on, Dar? Something has been off since the

equinox. I thought the potion mix-up had rattled you, but now I'm not so sure."

"Look, Prue, it's nothing just—"

"Don't lie to me, Darcee. Whatever it is, you can tell me. We're best friends."

Her blue eyes swim with compassion. Kindness washes over her face. I take in her dark hair that's braided loosely down her back. She wore it the same way at orientation five years ago. She singled me out to pair off, and we've been inseparable ever since. We'd share stories of our class crushes and gossip about the mean professors. We were roommates until we were approved for single dorms.

No one knows me better.

That is why I tell her everything. It all spills from my lips like a flood. I can't stop as I bare everything. From the moment I found Mistress Saege crying to the truth behind the sleeping dram mix-up. I tell her about Bael, what we've done together, and how I've come to care for him so much that I hope next week never ends.

When I am done, we are all alone on the path. Prue has remained silent during my whole tale. Her eyes widen slightly, and her mouth parts. She snaps it shut. The silence continues to stretch, and I squirm under her gaze.

"Say something. Anything," I beg. "Tell me how awful I am and that you're going to report me to the Head Mistress."

That snaps Prue out of whatever shocked stupor she was in. Blinking her eyes rapidly, she slightly shakes her head.

"I'd never do that, and you aren't awful." Her hand rests gently on my arm. "I think you made a foolish choice and acted rashly."

"I'm giving him an antidote and stopping whatever is between us."

"But you like him," Prue whispers.

I nod, a sad smile on my lips.

"More than I ever thought possible. More than I should."

"And if he takes the antidote and still wants you, would you try again with him?"

Foolish hope rises within me, but I know what will happen when he receives the cure. Fresh tears spring to my eyes.

"Oh, Prue, once he takes the antidote, he'll return to hating me—probably even more so now."

Biting her lip, Prue glances around, but we're still alone. We'll need to catch up with the group or be hopelessly lost. Her eyes land back on me as she shifts from foot to foot.

"Listen, you're my best friend who permitted me to read your aura, remember?"

I nod, confusion making my brows lower.

"One of the fundamental rules is that we aren't allowed to discuss one person's aura with another unless we get their consent. It's a very invasive thing to do," she says. "However, I'm willing to break that sacred covenant because I love you."

I can't help but grin.

"We are such bad witches," I giggle.

Prue's eyes dance with mirth.

"I know." She pauses, once again glancing behind her. "Maybe there is a chance for you and the High Warlock. After he takes the antidote."

"What do you mean? Prue, you remember how he always acted towards me. I was an annoyance at best."

Prue shakes her head.

"His aura was always black. Truthfully, I'd never seen one so dark before. And then occasionally—if I'd blink, I'd miss it—it would change when he'd look at or speak to you."

"Change how?" Dangerous hope causes my heart to race.

"It would—"

A shrill whistle cuts through the air. Both of us look up to see Zander quickly approaching. He has his thick-rimmed glasses on today. Maneuvering under the branch with ease, he stomps towards us. His expression is relieved as he looks over Prue and me.

"There you two are. We were wondering where you've been. The High Warlock is none too pleased you've fallen so far behind."

Prue casts me a glance, but I focus on Zander as he urges us further down the path. Zander goes under the branch first and holds it aloft for Prue. Her eyes bore into mine as she mouths, *later*, before ducking under the branch. Zander keeps it up for me, and we walk at a breakneck speed to catch up with the rest of the group.

The foliage turns darker. Creatures scurry along the ground and climb the trees to rustle in their leaves. The winding path and the setting sun make the woods seem more ominous.

I'm grateful when we break into a clearing. Up ahead is the rest of the group. Bael's eyes are wild, and a vein in his neck is throbbing. Concern is written in every line of his face. His hands twitch as if they seek to grab me. My heart melts a little —upset that I worried him when he couldn't come for me.

"Nice of you two to rejoin us." His voice is clipped, but I hear the relief in it all the same.

Prue and I stand shoulder to shoulder and take in our surroundings. A lone cottage sits a little ways up on a hill. Smoke billows from the chimney while a small pond sits next to it. It is a modest structure made of graying wood with a large garden at the back—Bael's home.

It's exactly as I would imagine it to be.

What would spending the night here be like instead of in my cramped dorm room? It feels like we are in another world this deep in the woods. If our relationship was real, I can imagine myself retreating here at the end of every evening. Bael and I would be living a simple life, spending our nights in each other's arms before we part in the morning for our jobs. It is a lovely dream—and will always remain just that.

With a wave of his hand, Bael gestures to the clearing around us.

"Now that we are all here, you should all pick a spot in this clearing to set down your packs and set up your tents. Once you have done so, please take your jars and hunt for the fungus while some light remains. A reminder that the mushrooms admit a poisonous gas after midnight and will need to be properly secured for storage."

Crossing his arms over his large chest, his expression remains serious.

"Once you have all collected your mushrooms, return here, where a light dinner will be served. We will spend the night here and then trek back to Axwyne in the morning."

There are a few snickers from the crowd as shoulders bump together. Bael pins each of us with a stare.

"I will remind you all that you're adults. I will not be doing tent checks. If there is an emergency, you may come to my cottage. Other than that, I trust you all to make good decisions and remind you that the creatures in these woods are nocturnal and always hungry. If you leave this clearing, my wards will not protect you from them."

A shiver goes through me. The students around me spring into action, and I look for a spot furthest away from the woods. Glancing over to my left, I notice Prue and Zande have set their tents up close to each other. Setting down my heavy pack, I sigh with relief. Fishing out my jar with the screw-top lid, I wave my hands over the rest of my belongings and watch my tent erect itself.

By the time I secure all my belongings inside, Prue and Zander are nowhere to be found. I'll need to speak to her and learn what she meant to tell me. Could there be hope for Bael and me once this is dealt with? I'm not counting on it. I'll give him the antidote and slip away as quickly as possible. Watching the tenderness in his gaze return to disdain will shatter my heart.

Picking up my jar and small harvesting bag, the setting sun helps me refocus on the task that's brought me here. The clearing empties quickly, and I do not know where to start looking. A cluster of students files into the woods directly behind my tent, and I follow them.

They move with ease through the overgrown trees. Stray branches catch my hair, and roots trip me—my bag of tools jingles with each step. The group I was following slowly gets eaten up by the thick trees, and it's not long before I'm walking with no clear direction.

Something slithers in the trees above me, and I nearly jump out of my skin. A furry creature scurries against my boot. I feel something lock around my arm, and I yelp, ready to smack whatever it is.

Violet eyes stop my movement. Bael's hand encases my elbow, and I relax. My eyes dart around us, but we are alone, entirely concealed by the dark trees.

"I was worried about you," he whispers. "I thought you had been—"

"I'm fine," I interrupt, my voice sharper than I mean it to be. My conversation with Prue has left me raw.

Bael lowers his brows, his eyes roaming my face before releasing my elbow.

"There's a stream up ahead," he says. "That's where you'll find most of the mushrooms."

"Thanks," I say, turning away from him and hurrying forward.

I pray he'll drop it and leave me alone, but he steps beside me. He guides branches out of my way and leads me down a path with smoother terrain. I say nothing, my thoughts racing. I should've done this from the beginning—push him away.

However, my plan to ignore him fails when he approaches me again.

"What's wrong?" he asks.

I don't meet his gaze.

"Nothing. Just eager to find this mushroom and get the fuck out of here."

His finger lifts my chin, forcing me to look at him.

"I know when you're lying to me, Darcee." He takes a step closer, our bodies brushing. The air turns heavy. "My backdoor will be unlocked this evening if you can escape the others."

My mind is all over the place. The unfairness of the situation spears its claws into my heart. I want him so badly, yet the only way to keep him is to give him the antidote that will make him hate me. The weight of the situation bears down on me, and my first instinct is to lash out.

"Is that all I mean to you?" I snarl. "A dirty little secret—no more than a toy you can play with and then hide back on the shelf."

Bael rears back at my anger. His fingers tighten on my chin.

"Firstly," he says, voice deepening. "The secrecy was your idea. I'd happily drag you into the middle of the clearing and fuck you in front of the whole class. I don't care who knows about us—I want everyone to know you are mine."

Madness dances in his gaze. I've glimpsed the primal part of him he alluded to in his office. Excitement dances through my blood and causes a dull ache between my thighs.

"I understand you want to wait until I am no longer your professor. But I won't have you thinking for even a moment, you mean so little to me. You are everything—I feel honored to have found you. Every moment with you is a gift I'll treasure for the rest of my life."

"Bael," I whisper. His candor steals my breath.

His body drifts closer to mine, his hand splaying along my back.

"I've wanted you for so long. Ever since—"

A twig snaps a few paces away, and we jump apart. Three students hurry past with their jars filled with mushrooms. They give us a passing hello before their footsteps get swallowed up by the woods.

Bael turns back towards me, but I take another step back.

"I'm going to collect the fungus and get out of here before it gets too dark. We'll talk later."

Bael nods, his lips grazing my forehead before he slips away. The shadows of the woods swallow him up. The sun is quickly fading, and by the time I hear the rushing of water, it's nearly completely set. My boots are caked in mood as I stomp to the end of the rushing stream. It smells putrid, like all the fish in it have suddenly died. The stench is nearly unbearable. Luckily, the silver glowing bodies of the *evernight mushrooms* are unmistakable.

Setting down my jar and opening my pack, I retrieve a small knife and tweezers and harvest the fungus. As I work, my thoughts drift back to Bael as they always seem to do these days. Every time we are together, his desire is palpable. It's hard to believe a potion—even created by a phenomenal love witch like myself—would craft such a deep connection. He alluded to wanting me for a long time, but that doesn't make sense. Love potions don't create false memories.

The more I give in to these heady moments with him, the more I risk the state of my heart once this is over. If there's one thing my family taught me, it is that those we love always hurt us the worst. It's unfair to put my past trauma on Bael—even more unjust that this relationship is one-sided, thanks to my irrational decision-making. I should be guarding my heart, but I've given it away freely to the one person who will undoubtedly break it.

I finish securing the top of my jar, which is nearly overflowing with mushrooms when something catches my eye.

Beyond the misty edge of the stream, something shimmers along the dark water's surface. An iridescent glow ripples from below. The sight transfixes me, and my body leans closer of its own accord.

That's when it strikes.

Oily tentacles shoot out from the surface of the water. I scramble back, but not quick enough. Slimy suckers wrap tightly around my calf and upper arm. Fire burns my skin as the monster secretes some sort of venom. A scream tears from my lungs as it pulls me towards the water. I'm flipped onto my stomach, mud splattering my face. I dig my free hand into the ground to try and save myself, but the mud is too slippery.

All I can do is scream and thrash as the creature drags me towards my watery death.

19

THE HIGH WARLOCK

Her scream rips through the forest and pierces his heart.

Why was he not watching closer? He would've sensed the beast's presence long before it could strike if he had. He had wanted to give her some space to think after she lashed out, but now he sees that was a mistake. Racing through the forest, he watches in horror as *the Kraken of the Bog* pulls her towards the murky water.

Her nails embed themselves into the ground, but the beast is too strong. Its tentacles encase her arm and leg, pulling them at odd angles. There is venom in the suckers, no doubt increasing her pain. Rage, unbridled and all-consuming, boils in his blood. The primal part of him, which he always keeps tucked away, rears its head.

Instincts drive him to protect her. The creature pulls her into the water, the lower half of her body already submerged. He races towards the water, his hand extended. Magic builds in his palm as he blasts the creature with purple fire. *The Kraken* recoils, tightening his grip on Darcee. Bael blasts it with his fire again, and the beast lets out a broken screech.

His tentacles release her onto the stream's banks as it slips below the surface. Bael charges towards her, pulling her shaking body into his arms. Her leg and arms are both bleeding. Red blood mixes with the green goo of the beast's venom. Darcee's pink lips are pale, and her teeth chatter.

He needs to get her back to camp so he can adequately tend to her wounds. Darcee continues to shudder. Her good arm curls against his chest, dragging him closer. Bael can hear footsteps off in the distance; they won't be alone much longer.

"Darcee." His hands drift up and down her shaking body. "Darcee, can you hear me?"

Magenta eyes blink up at him. They glow anew—looking at him like she never has before.

"You saved me," she whispers.

A fierceness pounds in his chest.

"Always," he vows. "I need to get you back and clean your wounds."

"You saved me," she repeats as if in a daze.

Leaning forward, her lips meet his without checking to see if they have an audience. He hates how cold they feel against him, but Darcee's mouth is always a delight. Scooping her into his arms, their mouths part, she rests her head against his shoulder.

Cradled in his arms, he carries Darcee past the curious students who break through the clearing. A few ask if she is alright, and he dismisses them. He needs to tend to her—he can't bear to see her in pain.

As he continues to walk with her, he feels it. He knew there was something different in how she looked at him, and now he has all the confirmation he needs. In the middle of *the Bog*, he feels the faintest flicker of her soul brushing his—something he's longed to feel for years.

His grip on her tightens—trying to capture it before it slips away.

No matter, he'll claim it and her before long. Darcee will be his forever.

20

DARCEE

You saved me.

The words ring repeatedly in my head as I sit around the small bonfire. The flames are burning low as no one has tended to it. Most students are back in their—or another's—tent for the evening. After making sure I was alright, Prue and Zander slipped away shortly after dinner.

I touch the bandage on my arm. Bael used his magic to clean me off before tending to my wounds. The salve he used burned, but he assured me it would kill any venom the creature may have tried to inject me with. I had felt dizzy and barely ate any of the simple stew served for supper. I glance up and see his small cottage outlined by the full moon.

His whispered promise in the woods tickles my ear.

Bael had been gentle with me as he healed me. His fear and worry had been palpable. His hand would squeeze mine more than once in comfort and reassurance that I was okay. I'm beginning to realize that he saved me in more than one way.

Sleep won't come easy tonight—not after what happened. I didn't think about packing my sleeping dram. Without it, I'll toss and turn as the memories of my past and tonight haunt me. I need to sleep. Bael said it was vital for me to rest to recover quicker.

The only way I will is if I seek him out tonight.

Rising from my spot at the fire, I quickly smother it with a flick of my wrist. The clearing is awash in darkness. I check to make sure no one is watching and walk on silent feet towards Bael's cottage. I slip through the open garden gate. Various herbs and midnight-blooming flowers perfume the air, making me forget we're in *the Bog*. My steps are quiet as I cut through the overgrown hedge. After a few paces, I stand before an old wooden door.

The brass knob turns, and the door swings open without a sound. Slipping inside, I find myself in the center of a modest kitchen. A teapot rests atop the stove. A few spice jars and root vegetables are stacked inside an old cabinet. It smells even more like Bael than his office does.

I feel like I've stepped into his life. My fingers trail over the scratched surface of his kitchen table. I can picture Bael here, cataloging herbs and crafting special potions. It's easy enough to imagine myself here as well—the two of us eating together. I'd have to add more pink decor to liven up the space. A small smile plays on my lips as I walk into the next room.

It is a small sitting area with a large loveseat and coffee table. Along the walls are bookshelves holding all manner of items. Displayed insects, skulls of various animals, and countless leather-bound books. Skimming over the spines, I feel the magic of the texts ripple through my hand.

I turn and find a small staircase. Above me is a loft glowing faintly with candlelight. A part of me whispers to turn back—going up there will change everything. I silence that tiny voice and give in to the selfish parts of myself that desire Bael's comfort above all else. I need to feel his closeness, hear his laugh, and let one of his stories lull me into a deep sleep.

I need him—a part of me always will.

The stairs creak under my weight as I slowly ascend them. Once I reach the top, my breath catches. The room is simple, consisting of a massive bed laden with black silk sheets and overstuffed pillows. Black and white pillar candles flicker around the room, giving the space just enough light for me to make out the figure in the center of the bed.

Bael rests against the headboard, his bare chest on full display. His violet eyes trace over my body, hardening when they get to my bandages.

"I didn't know if you'd come," he says softly.

"I almost didn't," I confess. "Things between us are moving so quickly. You don't know things about me—things I've done. I worry that it'll ruin what we have when you find out."

His eyes flash.

"Darcee, nothing you could have done will change how I feel about you." He holds out his hand to me. "When you are ready to share, I'll always be here."

A watery laugh escapes me.

"It all seems so simple. I wish it could stay that way."

I'd give anything for things to be different. We're running out of time, and I want to ensure he always has a piece of me when we part. I can't stop myself. When the potion has run its course, or he's ingested the antidote, he will always have this kernel of my heart and know how real it was.

My hands go to the hem of my fresh wool sweater and pull it over my head. The movement tugs at my sore arm, but I barely feel the discomfort. Stepping out of my shoes and socks, I drop my linen shorts on the floor. Bael's breathing turns ragged as I stick my thumbs into my panties and pull them down, leaving me completely naked.

"I know we cannot lie together, but I thought we could still get close tonight."

I walk towards his extended hand and allow him to pull me into his embrace. The familiarity of it brings tears to my eyes.

"Graduation can't come soon enough," he whispers.

I nod, even as fresh cracks splinter my heart.

I lift my head, and our lips connect. The kiss is tame, a gentle exploration of each other. His hands skim through my hair before falling to my back. Bael trails his palms up and down my spine, feeling every inch of my naked skin.

His palms freeze, and his whole body tenses. Our mouths part, and I stare into his hard eyes. I can feel the anger building inside of him.

"Who did this to you?" A quiet fury colors each word.

I've been so careful to keep him away from my back each time we've been together. He's never questioned it and is easy enough to distract if he ventures too close. Now, I've laid myself bare in his arms, ready to share more with him than anyone else.

I crawl up his chest, and our foreheads press together.

"My family wasn't supportive of my gifts. I was raised in a religious household—my parents are extremely devoted. So, when my magic began manifesting at age ten, they thought it was surely some devil's work. I'd been corrupted and was unclean. At first, when they'd catch me using my powers, I was reprimanded—forced to spend time alone in my room, no supper, things like that. It was verbal for the first few years. My father believed he could pray the disgraceful acts out of me. I'd beg for forgiveness for hours, but my magic grew stronger."

I swallow loudly. My eyes fall shut as if I can physically recoil from the memories. Bael's hands soothe me and guide my back to my body.

"When I turned sixteen, my father realized prayer wouldn't be enough. The devil inside me was strong and, therefore, would need a more severe remedy. That's when the reprimanding became harsher—more corporal."

"He beat you," Bael spits. I feel the slightest tremble in his hands.

I hadn't realized I began crying until I feel the tears rolling down my cheeks.

"The nightmares—I still have such terrible nightmares of the years I spent with them. Of being locked in that small closet. Dreading the moment, he opened it, knowing that pain would be on the other side. No matter what I did—no matter how many times I prayed to be different, this was who I was. And through it all, I loved them—a part of me always will—but it wasn't until I came across a flyer for Axwyne that I learned there was hope for me. Mistress Saege helped me get a scholarship after working my first year. Once I found my affinity for being a love witch, I was able to start making money of my own. I've saved nearly every coin I've earned to open my apothecary. I'll live in the little apartment above. It'll be hard work, but it's what I've always wanted."

Using the back of my hand, I wipe away my tears.

"I'll make it a success. Anything is better than going back to that place. Not that I'd think they'd have me. I've reached out to them over the years—even invited them to my graduation, hoping maybe something had changed—but I was foolish to do so. Their condemnation of me was swift and unflinching."

Bael is quiet as I finish telling him the story of my past. Sharing these memories with him lessens my burden. It helps me process just what I went through and see it for what it was. Violet eyes trace over my face, his sturdy presence never wavering. He doesn't pry—doesn't offer up advice to me or make some half-hearted attempt to relate. Bael simply holds me closer, his lips brushing over my forehead.

His fingers skim over each one of my scars, and I shiver. Something passes over his face, and I feel the same way. His full lips part, but I silence him with a kiss.

"Don't say it," I whisper against his mouth. "Not yet."

Even if I desperately want to hear those three words from

him, I can't. Not now, not ever. It'll only break my heart further when all of this is over.

Bael returns my kiss.

"I won't," he says. "Not until you're ready to hear it. Then I'll say it so much you'll grow sick of it."

I smile even as a familiar pain in my chest intensifies. Pulling back the sheets, I toss them aside and press open-mouth kisses against his chest.

"Let's not talk about the past anymore tonight," I say. "I want to feel you—see you."

His growl vibrates against my lips. In a flash, he's rolled me onto my back, his mouth landing on mine in a clash of tongue and teeth. He's become the most perfect kisser. His lips are firm yet gentle. He tastes of spice. Large hands cup my breasts, molding them roughly before tweaking my nipples.

My hips rise from the mattress to wrap my legs around his waist. The hardness concealed by his silk pants makes me squirm. My hands reach down, seeking his waistband.

"Let me see you," I beg. "All of you."

Bael growls into my mouth but nods. Together, we work his pants down until he is just as naked as I am. My mouth goes dry at the sigh of his cock. The shaft is gray and decorated with veins before giving way to a dark head. The length and size of him make my thighs clench. How I'd love nothing more than to feel him stretching me—burying himself so deep there would be no separating us. I have no doubt I'd feel him every time I moved the next day.

"Bael," I sigh.

My fingers itch to touch him, but I hold back.

His mouth leaves mine to kiss down my jaw. The wet glide of his tongue swirls around my throat. He kisses lower, stopping to taste each of my nipples until they are in tight peaks. Then he drifts lower, dipping the wet muscle into my naval before skimming his nose over the light dusting of pink hair between my thighs.

Warm breath tickles my most intimate flesh. His hands land on my hips, dragging me closer to his mouth. His heavy cock bobs as he slides down the bed. Knowing I'll never get to feel it makes me delirious. I'm desperate for more—to imagine what it would be like to have him.

"Tell me what you want to do to me." My hands settle atop his on my waist. "When you make me yours—I want to know how you'll do it."

Bael groans against my pussy. He gives me a slow lick as if desperate for a taste.

"I would bring you back here. I'd take you up to my bed and strip you out of whatever frilly outfit you'd have on. It'd be pink, of course."

His tongue licks my clit, and I gasp.

"Then what?" I ask, my voice trembling.

"I'd kiss you until you were blushing—turning pink in all the right places." I feel a finger tuck into my entrance, making my hips begin to writhe. "I'd have to have a taste before we went too far. First, I'd feast on your perfect breasts—then I'd move lower. Devouring your sweet little cunt until you couldn't take it anymore."

A moan falls from my lips at his crude language. The wet glide of his tongue mixes with my arousal. It slips down my legs and is soaking the sheets below me. A flush spreads across my chest as my muscles tighten.

"Then what would you do?" I pant.

"Then," he pauses and raises his head. His lips are glossy with my arousal. "I'd come down on top of you and pin you to the center of my bed.

Another finger adds to the one thrusting inside of me. He scissors them in a way that has my toes curling into the mattress. Stars begin to dance in my vision.

He licks me over and over, my peak looming closer when he stops. Bael rises onto his knees. My legs fall around his hips. Gripping his hard cock in his hands, he slaps it against my clit, causing my whole body to jerk. The head looks painfully large.

"Then, little witch, I'd stare into your eyes as I slid inside of you. Your tight little pussy would grip me just right." He slides his cock through my wetness before rubbing it against my clit again. "I'd fuck you over and over again until you screamed my name."

The hardness of his cock thrusts over my clit again and again. My muscles tighten at the feel of him. Like this, it is easy to picture him doing everything he's been describing. His hands land on either side of my head. My fingers curl around his straining forearm.

"I'd feel you come on my cock and listen as you begged for me to come inside of you. Only once I was sure you'd had enough would I finally find my release."

"Oh, Goddess," I moan.

"And you know what I'd do next, little witch?"

I thrash on the bed, my climax closing in on me. The muscles of his chest tighten as he continues thrusting. Just one more brush of his cock, and I'm done for. Bael's head dips into the crook of my shoulder, and his lips find my ear.

"I'd lift your hips and watch my seed drip out of your pink cunt."

A scream tears through me. Pleasure erupts from deep within my soul. My pussy clamps around nothing. Fresh arousal flows out of me and soaks the sheets below. Bael squeezes the head of his cock, a choked groan coming from him before he falls back to the mattress.

Licking me clean, Bael growls against my flesh as he goes. My body trembles long after he is done. The aftershocks of pleasure zip through me. I feel him come down beside me and place a kiss on my sweaty brow. He curls me into him and covers us with the silk sheet.

The silence stretches in the dark before Bael breaks it.

"I will give you space until graduation—my control is slipping as is, and I want to honor your wishes to wait."

My hands curl into his chest.

"Will you still hold me while I sleep? You're the only thing that keeps the nightmares away."

It's selfish to ask, but when have I been anything but where Bael is concerned?

He smiles down at me.

"Of course, little witch. Our tutoring session will go back to being chaste as well. You have another test to take this week before your final exam."

I sigh, content, and cuddle deeper into his warmth. A sense of completion overwhelms me. Silently, I pray to the Goddess that everything will be as it should be. If we are meant to, Bael and I will find our way back to each other. There is no point denying it anymore, especially not after tonight.

I love him. I don't know the exact moment it happened, but it's true—I'm in love with Bael. Right now, he loves me too. He said nothing would ever make him turn from me, but I know that isn't true. It can't be.

Exhaustion weighs me down. I don't need to ask my tarot cards to know a broken heart is in my future.

21

———

DARCEE

The week following the trip to *the Bog* passes in a blur. School ramps up as final exams are handed out and term grades are received. In each of my courses, I passed with flying colors. Yesterday, I retook the third exam in Bael's office and obtained a satisfactory score. With the threat of failing his class no longer looming, there is only one last thing to do.

I glance up at the clock on the wall. Our final necromancy class is almost over, and I'm the last one to complete the *Dead Man's Elixir*. I can feel the eyes of the other students on me, as well as Bael's heavy stare. I don't dare look up at him and lose my focus.

The heavy stone cauldron bubbles away on my desk. Thick steam curls over the pot's dark lip. The scent is a mix of mint and fresh soil. I slice through the *evernight mushroom* with trembling hands and drop it into the brew. I hold my breath in anticipation. After a moment, the liquid turns sparkling blue, and I quickly add the last bit of crushed herbs.

Using a wooden spoon, I stir the potion seven times clockwise and ten times counterclockwise. Dousing the flame, I pick up the glass dropper on my desk and fill it with the reanimation potion. The dead raven on my desk lays still atop a metal tray. I insert the tweezers into its beak and gently open it wide enough to trickle in some of my brew.

It should only take a few drops.

I hold my breath, anticipation building in the room. The blood rushing in my ears makes it so I can barely hear. *Come on, I will it. Wake up, little bird.*

There is the softest fluttering of atrophying feathers. The first movement is jerky—disjointed—then the creature lets out a raspy squawk and jumps up. It tests its bald wings before launching into the air and taking a meandering lap around the room. My eyes widen in shock, barely believing what I'm seeing. Once it lands back on my desk, its whole body tenses before falling limp to the tray with a clatter.

I let out a squeal of delight and clap my hands. A few other students join in, and I turn to the left and embrace Prue. She hugs me back tightly with a delighted giggle. We break apart, and my eyes go to Bael. There is pride swimming in his violet gaze. He scrolls something on the parchment before him, a secretive smile on his lips that is only for me. I stare down at my final grade and grin.

I passed—that's it, I'm going to graduate.

Smiling up at him, he gives me a short nod. If we were alone, he'd be much more vocal with his praise. That's one of the things I've missed. He's been true to his word about keeping his distance. Still, he comes to my bed each night, holding me close before disappearing in the early morning. Our tutoring sessions have now come to an end. I long for his affection, but I know this is for the best.

We have arranged to meet after the graduation ceremony and spend the evening together. It is then when I will give him the antidote. We'll be at his cottage, far enough away from everyone that I'll slip away without facing the consequences of what I've done. I am a coward.

After class, I'm working on the antidote so it has enough time to charge over the weekend. It'll need to be robust to counteract the love potion.

Glancing down at my passing grade, I wonder if it was worth all of this. Yes, I am one step closer to my dream of opening an apothecary, but for the first time in my life, the idea no longer seems as appealing—not when it means giving up Bael to have it. Yet I know I cannot keep him.

The bell rings, and I quickly collect my things. A few students hang back to bid Bael farewell. Our eyes meet, and I wish I could stay, but I have an antidote to brew. Prue and I file out together. I've barely seen her since *the Bog*—undoubtedly because she and Zander took things to the next level in their tent that night.

I do not wish to hear whatever she tried to tell me in the woods. My mind is made up, and I don't need traitorous false hope to make it any worse. Prue bumps my shoulder as we walk, and I look at her.

"How have things been? Zander and I can barely keep our hands off each other." Prue cringes, her face paling. "Sorry, you probably don't want to—"

"Love witch, remember? Of course, I want to hear! I'm so happy for you, truly." My throat tightens. "The only person to blame for my unhappiness is myself."

Prue's lips drop into a frown.

"I've never seen you like this, Dar. So sad." She touches my shoulder gently. "Look, what I was going to say at *the Bog*—"

"I don't want to hear it—not right now, Prue. Okay?" The words rush from my mouth. I gently shake off her touch. "I—I have to go."

I don't wait for her response and hurry down the hallway. The walls seem to be closing in on me. The painful ache in my chest yawns open, slicing at my soul with its claws. What's the point of anything when I can't have the one thing I truly desire? There will never be another who makes me feel like Bael does, and I've ruined it. This whole mess is my fault.

Bursting into Saege's room, I get to work without giving myself a chance to reconsider making it. I remember the spell I used, plucking which ingredients will counteract them the best. I toss them all into a cauldron. Closing my eyes, I pull at my warm magic, allowing the golden light to flow from me and into the brew. With it, I set my intention to undo what I've done—infusing it into the concoction.

Once I open my eyes, I stare down at the magenta liquid. I stir it vigorously to make sure everything is incorporated. One vial of this and all the love Bael has shown me these past weeks will be done for. I'll be alone again, but only this time will I have the memories of what could've been to contend with. They gather around the room, hiding like shadows and sneering at me.

A choked sob works its way up my throat. My tears drench the table below. Droplets fall into my potion, causing it to shimmer. I quickly turn the flame off and push it away.

"Darcee?" A concerned voice calls from above. "Is that you?"

Furiously, I wipe at my face.

"Yes, Mistress Saege. I'm down here."

My voice sounds raw.

Saege appears in one of her long white silk robes. Her graying hair is pulled into a loose bun at the base of her neck, and a pencil protrudes through it. Gracefully, she floats over to me, her eyes rife with concern.

"My dear, whatever is the matter?"

I shake my head, trying my best to fake a convincing smile.

"Nothing, Mistress. It's just graduation blues. I'm going to miss this place—more than I thought."

Saege nods, but I know my lie does not entirely convince her.

"You don't have to leave at all. We'd be happy to have you join us as faculty here. Love magic has been missing from the curriculum for some time. We haven't had as fine a love witch as you in decades."

My heart lifts at her praise. In a perfect world, I take her up on the offer. I'd consider giving teaching a go recently. Love magic is so woefully underappreciated. Bael and I could work side by side, spending nights together in his cottage and passing each other in the hall—sneaking off for midday trysts while no one was watching.

It is a lovely dream that cannot be.

"Thank you, Mistress Saege, but I've already paid for my first month's rent at the apothecary."

"If you ever change your mind, the offer still stands." Saege begins to turn before pausing. Her eyes are so intense I almost buckle under her stare. "Forgive me for prying, my dear. However, I wonder if some of your distress has to do with Professor Fangborne."

My mouth goes dry, and I have to grip the side of the table to stay upright. I search for the words, not finding any of use. Saege waves a dismissive hand.

"You're an adult, Darcee. Besides, the fraternization policy between students and professors is murky at best."

I don't want to lie to her, so I let my silence be all the confirmation she needs. Saege nods, a smile playing on her lips.

"That's how these things always go, isn't it? Opposites attract. As I'm sure you know, Bael is a good male." Her eyes harden. "Unless he's done something horrible to you that I must be made aware of."

I shake my head.

"He's the best male I've ever known."

Saege's smile deepens.

"What he did for me and my brother is a kindness most would not offer. Going in the veil like that takes a toll, but he knew how much I'd been suffering."

All of this started because I believed him to be horrible—capable of nothing but cruelty. How wrong I had been. The true male Bael is will make the perfect partner for someone, and as much as I wish that person were me, it won't be. Fresh tears threaten to spill from my eyes, but I wipe them away.

"Why the tears then, my dear?"

"Everything is just happening so fast—I—"

"That is the nature of love, isn't it? You would know better than anyone how all-consuming it can be. It's the most powerful magic in the world." Her smile turns wistful. "I don't know why I'm even surprised. He was always so enamored with you."

The blood in my veins freezes.

"What do you mean?"

Mistress Saege gives a delicate shrug.

"Bael was always asking after you—practically from the moment you arrived. Then, when you became my teaching assistant, he'd constantly pepper me with questions about you and your skill level. He was always impressed by your proficiency in divination and potion making." Saege chuckles softly. "It's why I suggested you enroll in his course—so he could finally experience you firsthand. Pretty good matchmaking on my part for a non-love witch, hmm?"

I would laugh along with her, but I feel unsteady. Traitorous hope rises within me no matter how hard I shove against it. I remind myself that curiosity and desire are not the same thing. Any interest he may have had in me before never prompted him to treat me with anything other than disdain.

Saege's warm hand falls to my shoulder.

"You deserve to be happy, Darcee. Besides, you won't be the first student-teacher relationship Axwyne has brought together.

The Head Mistress and I met when I was a student, and we've been together for decades."

I give her a watery smile.

"I hope our love is as everlasting as yours."

Saege squeezes my shoulder before turning away.

I gaze down at the antidote brewing in my cauldron. The cracks in my heart deepen as I stare into it. I have to give him this if there is even the slightest chance of us having a future. We'll find each other if we are truly meant to be. And if we aren't well, I'll be glad that I'm far enough away from him when the potion wears off, and I won't see the fondness on his face twist into disgust.

Sticking to my plan should be easy enough. I'll be gone before he even realizes what I've done.

22

THE HIGH WARLOCK

He holds her in his arms the morning of graduation. Counting her deep breaths, he lets the feeling of her warm body soothe the frayed edges of his nerves. It has been agony waiting, but the pain was worth it. Keeping away from her had nearly been impossible. Now he knows he will never be apart from her again after tonight.

It's what he's wanted from the first moment he saw her at student orientation five years ago. The young woman with magenta eyes and round cheeks. He'd never felt so drawn to another in his life. Keeping close watch over her through the years had been delicious torture. For years, he'd scan his class list hoping to see her name, but their paths had no reason ever to cross.

And then, at the beginning of this semester, everything had come alive when he saw Darcella Thistle printed on the ledger for his introductory to necromancy course. From that first day, some part of him knew they would end up here—together like this. The fact that she also wants him is a revelation—one he will always cherish for the rest of their lives.

His restless soul reaches toward hers. When he is inside her tonight—claiming her as his mate—they will finally become one. Two halves will reunite with the sacred promise of forever. He loves her. The High Warlock has felt this way for a very long time. Seeing her with another at the equinox party snapped something inside of him.

He had wasted enough time, and if he didn't act soon, he could lose her forever—something he would never forgive himself for doing.

Dawn breaks inside her small dorm. Most of her belongings are packed tightly into boxes. Wherever she goes, he will always follow. Today is when their life together begins.

The bare walls of her room glisten in the morning light. Inhaling the scent of her hair deeply, he presses a lingering kiss to her forehead.

"Tonight," he vows in her ear.

She stirs slightly as he leaves her warm body but remains fast asleep. With one last lingering look, knowing she'll finally be his tonight makes leaving her a bit easier. His magic flows through him, and he quickly transforms into a raven.

Leaping from the window, he flies directly towards the rising sun.

23

DARCEE

"Darcella Thistle!" announces the Head Mistress.

With a smile—and walking slowly so as not to break my neck in my pink heels—I cross the graduation stage. The wide brim of my witch's hat shades my eyes from the evening sun. Mistress Saege holds out my wand and protective case, which I accept with my diploma, proclaiming me an Axwyne School of Magic graduate.

She quickly hugs me before the next name is called, and I'm passed down the line. Shaking hands with each staff member, my palm tingles when my eyes meet a familiar violet pair. Bael is beaming with pride. I quickly move down to the next professor lest I burst into tears in the middle of the congratulation line.

The promise of tonight burns like an inferno between us. One that will be extinguished soon enough.

My parents had not shown up, and I'm finally okay with never seeing them again. After I confessed to Bael, I've been considering talking to someone regularly about what I went through. I'm tired of being afraid of my past. Everything I endured under the cruel hands of my father made me think Bael could be just like him.

Now I know that couldn't be farther from the truth.

The rest of the ceremony moves quickly. A large bonfire is lit in celebration, and we all toss our pointed hats into the air. Fireworks light up the sky as sweet-smelling smoke billows around us. The sun is already lowering by the time I make it out of the crowd.

I spy a familiar dark head and embrace my best friend. She looks gorgeous in her black dress with blue beading. We grip each other tightly, shaking with tears and excitement.

Pulling back, I blink away the moisture in my eyes.

"How are we gonna go from seeing each other every day to every *other* day?" I ask.

Prue laughs. She'd told me shortly before the ceremony that Zander and she were getting a place near me in the next town over. He would be an apprentice at the local library while she worked under the local charms master.

"Somehow, we'll manage."

Her parents appear and hug us both. Her mother is just an older version of Prue, while her father has a short, stocky build and a thick white beard. His laugh is booming as he embraces me.

"Congratulations, girls!" he cheers. "Now, Prueitt Starlow, it's time you introduce us to this boyfriend of yours."

I laugh at her jovial father, trying his best to look stern. Prue also chuckles before leading them away and waving goodbye to me over her shoulder. My heart lifts—delighted that my friend has found her happy ending. I watch them go, my heels sinking into the soft grass below me. A lone breeze picks up around me, tugging at the slit hem of my short dress.

A familiar presence presses against my side. Taking a deep breath, I turn and find Bael behind me. The setting sun casts his face in harsh shadows. He's standing too close to me, but that matters little now. A million thoughts race through my head as I stare up at him. With today's excitement, putting this evening out of my mind has been easy. The bag on my shoulder feels heavy, with the antidote resting inside.

"Congratulations," he whispers.

I will the tears not to form in my eyes as I stare up at him. Heat races up my neck, and my throat feels tight. Bael merely leans down, his lips finally finding my ear.

"Are you ready for your gift?"

I smile as he pulls back from me.

"I've been waiting my whole life for it."

Bael chuckles, his eyes glancing around the crowded lawn.

"This party has far too many people. I want you all to myself."

Heat swims in my cheeks as I glance around as well. Something tickles my neck, and I turn to the side. My eyes meet those of Romina. Her gaze is narrowed, having witnessed Bael and I's interaction. It's a juvenile thing to do, but I feel my lips pull into a smirk anyway.

Turning back to him, I push up on my toes and bring our mouths together. He sighs against my lips, his hand splaying against my back and dragging me closer. We part for air, and my eyes find Romina's again. Her face is a picture of quiet furry. If looks could kill, I'd drop dead in an instant.

Taking Bael's hand in mine, I forget all about her and grin up at him.

"I was thinking the same thing."

Bael leads me out of the courtyard and towards his cottage. The overgrown woods are easy to navigate, with him leading me—even in heels. The terrain remains flat, and he holds the branches I need to duck under. The sun has fully set, and a large blue moon glows above his cottage. The woods are quiet tonight as we get to his home and enter through the front door.

I can imagine myself walking home with him every night.

We'd dine together and make love upstairs until exhaustion claimed us. Then we'd go to work and start the evening ritual again. The image is so vivid it's like I've lived it.

The door clicks shut behind us, and Bael moves quickly. His lips find mine again. The desperation in his kiss tells me the waiting has been just as painful for him. He molds me to him, my stomach pressing against his hard cock. I groan into his mouth, my hands sliding into his silky hair. I commit every detail to memory, knowing this will be the last time I feel his lips on mine.

His lips skim down my jaw, licking and biting as he goes. Pausing to tease the sensitive skin of my neck, my head falls back. Resting on the small coffee table is a box wrapped in purple velvet, tied with a matching ribbon.

"What's that?" I sigh, needing to find some way to break the kiss before I let it go too far.

Bael glances over, and I watch the gray skin of his cheeks darken. Slowly—almost sheepishly—he walks towards the box. Lifting it in his hands, it rattles as he extends it towards me.

"Your graduation gift."

My lips twist.

"I thought you had something else in mind."

"Trust me, little witch, that's still happening." Ice forms over my heart at the heat in his gaze. "I wanted to give this to you first."

I take the box from him, and its weight is surprising. Carefully, I unwrap the soft fabric. It is a wooden case with golden hinges. I unlock it and nearly drop it to the floor—a gasp echoes in the quiet room. Rows of glittering gold coins sparkle up at me in the candlelight.

Bael walks over, his gaze burning.

"This should help cover the rent of your apothecary for the next few years," he explains in a rush.

"At least," I whisper. "This—Bael—this is too much. I can't accept it."

"Please, Darcee. I have more than enough money." His hand cups my cheek. "I know there are a million conversations we need to have about the future, but I want us to be together from this moment forward. Wherever you choose to be is where I'll be, too. I've already given Axwyne my notice. My life is yours now—as is my money."

"Bael..."

I trail off, not knowing how to find the words.

"Don't say anything," he says, as if reading my thoughts. "I want you to be happy, Darcee. To be fulfilled in whatever way you want. You haven't had an easy go of things, and I'd be honored to help provide at least some part of your dream."

Oh, how I love this male. Goddess, I love him so much it burst from my heart and soul. He will always have me—no amount of time or distance will undo what has happened between us. Try as I might to protect my heart, I gave it to him from the first day.

I have to end this. Now.

Closing the box lid, I rise to kiss him.

"Thank you," I say—never agreeing to take the money.

I set the box down on the table and reach into my bag. My hands graze over the smooth glass shape of the wine bottle and pull it out.

"We should celebrate with a drink."

Bael nods. "I'll get some glasses."

I stop him with a hand on his arm.

"Allow me."

Quickly, I shuffle into the kitchen and locate two wine glasses. I fish through my bag and find the small vial of antidote. I pour it into the left glass before uncorking the wine bottle. The dark liquid should conceal the potion. Taking a deep, shuddering breath, I return to the room.

My body goes numb, and I plaster a fake smile on my face. I hand him his tainted glass, and we clink them together cheerfully. Taking a smile sip, he wrinkles his nose.

"Bitter," he says.

I need him to drink all of it to ensure it works. The air around us shifts as his hand goes to my waist—his warmth seeps through the thin material of my pink dress. I go into myself, preparing for one final performance and hoping to make it through without shattering.

"I liked how you kissed me in front of everyone," he purrs.

"What can I say? I'm full of surprises."

I cup the back of his hand, my thumb grazing over his soft skin, savoring the feel of it for the last time. I gently lift it from my hip and slide it along the outside of my thigh. The hem of my dress rises as I drag his hand along my bare skin. His breathing turns ragged as his fingers brush the lacy strap of my thong high on my hip.

"Finish your wine and go upstairs," I command with a grin. "I have another surprise I want to show you."

Bael shivers before downing the rest of his wine in one swallow. I collect his empty glass, and he leans down, kissing me fiercely. His tongue seeks mine for one final pet before he pulls back.

"How did I get so lucky to find you?"

I smile at him as he turns, unbuttoning his black silk shirt. Once the stairs stop creaking and I hear him settle on the bed, I move quickly. Pulling the crumpled piece of parchment from my pocket, I tuck my pathetic excuse of an apology under his thoughtful gift.

The coins would provide me with a comfortable future where money was never a worry again. I glance up at the loft and the love I'm losing forever. The idea of the apothecary and spending my life helping others find love with my eternally broken heart nearly makes me fall to my knees. Tears burn in my eyes, but I cannot let him hear me cry.

Quietly slipping off my heels, I walk back into the kitchen and collect my bag. The backdoor is just as silent as the first time I used it. I slip out into the garden. The scent of herbs and fresh flowers fills my lungs. The stars and moon glow overhead as the silence of the woods engulfs me. I take a deep breath, reaching for my magic and using it to transform into the only other creature I've ever been able to manage.

Once I am a magenta butterfly, my thin wings flap with all their might away from Bael and the life I could've had. I don't stop until Axwyne is a spect in the distance and my new town comes into view.

The old apothecary needs a fresh coat of paint. Luckily, the previous tenants left behind most of their inventory, so I'm not having to stock it from scratch. It's little more than a room with three rows of wooden shelves, a counter, and a small office in the back I'll use for love readings.

I flutter up to the next level and transform back into my body once inside my small apartment. Again, it's nothing special. My boxes still need to be unpacked. The walls are bare. The small kitchen is along one wall, and my unmade bed rests on the other. With some time, I can make this room into a home.

The task seems overwhelming. I go to the nearest box marked bedding and rip it open. Pulling out a pillow and my quilt, I toss them onto the bed. Unzipping my dress, I feel the weight of the past two weeks crashing down on me. Completely naked, I slide under my old blanket. Bael's scent still clings to the fibers, and fresh tears spill down my cheeks.

The only way I'll sleep tonight is if I exhaust myself. So I sob into the pillow, the moonlight streaming in from my broken window. Bael may come looking for me. Only Prue and

Mistress Saege know where I've gone off to. Surely, they won't betray my location if he is as angry as I suspect he will be.

I'm such a coward. I should've stayed to face him and holdfast in the face of his wrath. If only I could see him one final time and leave with some awful version of him, perhaps that would make my broken heart less painful. As it stands now, the rough shards of it tear at my skin until I'm bleeding.

Loneliness yawns open inside of me. It swallows me whole, and I succumb to my misery. All that I've lost flashes through my mind. The memories of Bael—his passion, his kindness, and his warmth—flood me. Each one cuts me a little deeper.

Maybe I don't have any business opening up this apothecary and offering my love services. After all, I can't be that good of a love witch, seeing how my own love potion broke my heart.

24

THE HIGH WARLOCK

She's been down there far too long, his little witch.

Gods, was there ever anyone or anything as beautiful as her? As kind and compassionate and feisty? He'll never stop being in awe of her. The ease with which she teases him and he teases her back. It contrasts sharply with the male he's always known himself to be.

She brings a lightness to him—a softness reserved only for her.

They hadn't made any plans for the future, but surely, she knew that after tonight, they would always be together. When he was finally buried inside of her, her fate would be sealed. Their lives would be bound together for eternity. Wherever she goes, he goes. Besides, opening an apothecary is no easy thing—especially all alone.

He'll help her in whatever way she'll allow. The need to take care of her is overwhelming.

Anticipation makes him restless. Minutes trickle by as he remains alone in his bed. What could she be doing down there? He had felt the lace of her panties—his fingers still smelt like her. It does not take her this long to shed her clothes and join him. Perhaps he is just too eager. Yet, as all remains still down below, something prickles his skin.

"Darcee?" he calls. Only silence greets him.

He jumps from the bed and crawls down the stairs to the main floor. She's no longer there. Nor is she in the kitchen or out in the garden. Could something have happened to her? Had someone broken in and stolen her when he was merely a floor away? It seems unlikely, and yet—

He's walking back into the den when he spies it. A lone piece of parchment is tucked under the box of coins he'd given her. Her familiar handwriting spells his name. He snatches it. Dread curdles his stomach as he reads.

"Bael, I'm sure the antidote has worked by now, and you realize what I've done. I never meant to slip you that love potion at the equinox. It was a terrible mix-up—one I let go too far. I should've come clean that morning in your classroom, but I felt drawn to you in a way I never have before. I've come to care for you while knowing what I did. I deserve your disgust—your hatred—and I'm too much of a coward to come clean to you in person. Please find it in your heart to forgive me, but I understand if you cannot. Everything was real to me. I'm sorry. Darcee."

A love potion? What is she talking about? The wine she gave him had been bitter, no doubt laced with whatever antidote she had given him. The note trembles in his grasp.

He feels no differently about her now than he always has. Is that what she thinks caused all of this? That he's been under the effects of a love potion, and that's why he sought her out?

When had she managed to slip him one on the equinox? Even if she had, it's not like it would—

He doesn't have time to dwell on her note. He needs to find her. Now.

Dropping the parchment, he seamlessly transitions into a raven and flies quickly toward her dorm room. The window is shut and locked, but he can see all he needs to from the ledge.

Her room is bare, and her bed is empty. He's a fool for not asking where her dream apothecary was—he'd thought she'd tell him after night.

It matters little. He'll find her. By any means necessary, his little witch will be his. And once he has her, there will be no doubt left in her mind just how much she means to him.

25

———

DARCEE

"And you haven't heard anything from him?" Prue asks.

She sits at the counter of my apothecary. Zander looks through a few of the shelves at the back, giving us space to chat. The shop is empty—just like it was yesterday. I need to find a better way of getting the word out that I'm open. I'll have to hire someone to add to the sign out front that love readings are now on offer.

I shake my head as I go back to filling small jars with dried rose petals.

"It's been two days. If he wanted to find me, he would've by now. That tells me all I need to know—he took the antidote, remember he hated me, and now I'll never see him again."

Prue shakes her head. Glancing to make sure Zander is out of earshot, she still drops her voice to a whisper.

"I know you didn't want me to tell you this before, but I'm telling you now."

"Even if I don't want to hear it?" I raise a brow.

Prue nods primly. I let out a heavy sigh, giving her my full attention.

"The High Warlock's aura never changed. During his lessons, it would always remain black—foreboding and not of this world. And then, for the briefest moments when he'd look at or speak to you, it would blaze pink. I didn't think much of it —only that maybe it was your natural power brushing up against him. Now, I wonder if there was more to it than that."

"When did you first notice it?"

"At the beginning of the semester. Weeks before the equinox party."

My heart begins to race. One final, traitorous thread of hope worms its way into my heart, trying to put back together the broken pieces.

"Well, this is all the proof you need to see it wasn't the case. He only felt what he did because of my potion."

Prue's lips twist, but thankfully, she drops it. I'm hoping we never have to speak of him again—it's too painful. The memories of our time together replace my nightmares. These past two nights, I've been waking up aching. My heart calls out to him but receives no answer.

"Prue, we should go if we're gonna make dinner," Zander says, coming to my friend's side.

Their love is palpable as she grins up at him. Rising from the stool, she grips my hand. We plan to catch up later this week, and I watch the two of them slip out my door and into the setting sun. I close in a few hours, and I'm not holding my breath for any new customers.

No matter. There's plenty of cataloging to keep me busy. Going from Axwyne, where people were always around, to living alone is quite the adjustment. The silence seems to stretch, and my mind can't focus enough to read a book in the evenings.

I pull out a few jars of dried bay leaves and orange peels. Leaving the desk, I search along the shelves, and find a couple of empty jars and my logbook. Bells chime at the front door, and a thrill goes through me. I smooth my hands on my smock and walk back through the shelves to greet my first customer.

"Welcome to Darcee's Apothecary of Love! Is there something I can help you with—"

The words die on my tongue as I round the corner and take in the figure standing at my door. Has he gotten more handsome? It seems impossible, but yet I can't deny it. His gray skin glows. His strong jaw is clenched. There are dark shadows under his violet eyes. Black satin covers him from head to toe.

Bael stares at me—his face unreadable.

I brace myself for his fury. He's only come here to rage against me—I know it. Even still, my heart lifts at the sight of him. I've missed him terribly. The ache in my chest starts anew. His spicy scent invades my lungs.

He takes a small step forward.

"There is a problem I was hoping you could help me with."

The slight tremble in his voice causes my throat to tighten. His eyes scan the shelves and the barren walls around me. This space suddenly feels very small, as if he's sucked all the air out of it.

"You see, I'm in quite the dilemma. There is this witch that left my company in quite a hurry." A muscle in his cheek ticks. "Didn't even say goodbye."

Misery weighs me down. I clear my throat, but my words still sound choked.

"I'm sure she had a good reason to."

Bael lets out a humorless chuckle.

"Oh, she believed she did. You see, this little witch is under the impression she slipped me a love potion, and that's the only reason I feel anything for her."

His heavy steps echo along the hardwood floor. I try not to move as he closes in on me. The breath saws out of my lungs. His body is close enough to touch mine. I hold my breath as his hand cups my cheek. Swallowing my moan at the feeling of his skin against mine, I lose myself in his gaze.

"However, it seems she's forgotten one vital thing about me?"

"What's that?" I whisper.

His full lips curl into a grin.

"That my kind are immune to all poisons, brews, and, most assuredly, love potions."

Shock covers me in cold water. What is he saying? How could he possibly be—and then I remember—a whisper of a memory of us in his office. Him drinking the nightshade tea even though it was still poisonous. He had been fine. He told me such things don't affect him.

That means—oh Goddess—that means he—

"I guess what I'm really asking for," he continues, "is if you have something that will make the most beautiful, compassionate, fiery witch I've ever met understand just how much I love her."

My control snaps as I launch myself into his arms. He stumbles back, and we clatter to the wooden floor. I pin him beneath me, joy overflowing from my soul. It's strong enough to knit back together the jagged pieces of my heart. The broken organ is whole once more and stronger than ever.

I rain kisses all over his face as he laughs beneath me. His chuckle heats my blood. Planting my palms on either side of his face, I stare down at him, panting.

"You must think I'm a fool," I say.

His eyes sparkle. "I don't think you are anything less than wonderful."

"I love you too," I say. "So much."

His lips connect with mine as his hands fall to the back of my legs. They run up and down my frilly skirt. Our kiss is a gentle exploration as if our mouths are getting reacquainted with each other. He tastes delicious. My body settles atop his fully, sealing our fronts together.

"How did you find me?" I ask, breaking our kiss.

"By giving Mistress Saege a very persuasive argument. She finally relented where you'd gone once she was assured of my undying love for you this afternoon."

A flush heats my cheeks. I rest my chin on his chest.

"I am sorry. I should've come clean immediately and shouldn't have left without explanation. I figured you'd hate me once you learned what I had done. Never could I have imagined you felt the way you do for me. I thought I was an annoyance at best to you."

Bael cringes, his whole body tensing beneath me.

"Then you must think I'm a fool, too." He curls a piece of my hair around his finger. "At first, you unsettled me. I'd never felt the way I do towards you about anyone. I'd been watching you for years—keeping tabs on you from a distance. Then, that night at the equinox, when I saw you with someone else, I realized I couldn't hold back anymore. If I wanted you, I had to act. It all flooded out once I fully embraced those feelings—so strong I couldn't stop it."

That day in detention, I had wrongfully perceived his appearance as being under the influence of my love potion. In reality, he had just been in love with me. Those symptoms weren't simulated—they were real.

I smile as my mouth comes down on his once more. His fingers tunnel into my hair as he holds me close. Our kisses turn rougher. His tongue gently plays with mine as my thighs slide to the other sides of his hips. Bael's head falls back, and his eyes are serious.

"Who had you meant to give the love potion to that night?"

Biting my lip, I shake my head—time to come fully clean.

"I hadn't meant to give it to anyone. I brewed it for Prue and

Zander—I accidentally mixed it up with a sleeping dram I was going to use on you."

His brows furrow.

"That day, I found Mistress Saege crying, and she said you were responsible for it. This was coming on the heels of me failing another test and realizing my ability to pass your class was dwindling. I was so angry—I made a plan to slip you a sleeping potion so that I could graduate and get revenge for Mistress Saege." I shake my head. "I thought you were cruel. I wanted you gone. Shortly after I had slipped it into your glass when I *accidentally* fell into your arms, I learned that they were tears of joy you brought Saege. As for my grade, I realize I should've just come to you for help."

Bael chuckles softly. His eyes turn serious.

"You know—come to think of it—after you fell into me, I didn't even drink my wine. I tossed it before returning to my cottage." His hands tighten on my backside. "The feeling of you in my arms was too overwhelming."

I giggle before sobering.

"No more lies. No more secrets. Just the truth from now on," I vow.

"Always," he agrees.

Gathering me to his chest, he rises with me in his arms. My legs wrap around his waist as I hear the apothecary door lock. Anticipation makes me shiver. His forehead falls to mine.

"Darcee, you must understand, if we lie together tonight, that is it for me. It will cement our bond—you will become my mate—and our lives will be tied together. My immortality will end, and I'll live as long as you do. We will be one in heart and soul. Is that what you want?"

I stare into his earnest gaze. Only an hour ago, I felt alone—resigned to spending the rest of my days toiling away at bringing other people together. Now, the Goddess has smiled upon me, bringing the love of my life back to me. Loneliness no longer lingers around me. There is so much warmth radiating from my heart that I can hardly breathe. For the first time in my life, I feel whole.

And it's all thanks to Bael.

"More than anything," I say.

A feral grin curls his mouth.

"Good, because if I don't get inside your little pussy soon, I'm going to die."

I capture his lips once more.

He growls against me. Our kiss never falters as he walks us up the short staircase to my apartment above. The door flies open and bangs against the wall. The setting sun makes the room darker. Candles blaze to life all around us. Thankfully, I made my bed this morning, and Bael tosses me into the center of it.

I push up on my elbows as he stares down at me. His breathing ragged as he lowers to his knees.

"You are my madness. Forever," he snarls.

His hands go to the zippers on my boots, gently dragging them down before shucking them off me. He removes my socks before reaching for the waistband of my skirt. I help him by pulling the sweater over my head and tossing it on the floor. Warm palms slide up my outer thighs and hips. Hooking his fingers into the sides of my panties, he pulls them off while I throw my bra to the floor.

Cupping each knee, he props me up until I am fully exposed to his hungry gaze. I've never felt this bare before. While I've been naked around him countless times, this feels different somehow. It's like he's seeing me—all of me for the first time. There are no more secrets between us, exactly how it should always be.

He raises and comes down on top of me. My hands go to his shirt, unbuttoning it as he kisses my jaw. Once the smooth muscles of his back are exposed to my hands, I trace over them.

Velvety soft skin tickles my hard nipples. My fingers slide lower on his back and slip under his pants to cup his firm backside.

"Naughty little thing you are."

"Are you going to make me beg?" I ask, batting my lashes.

"Not yet."

Tongue and teeth mash together as I fumble to the front of his pants for the button. Once it's opened, I slide his zipper down and help him shuck his last piece of clothing. Our naked skin rubs together. His warmth settles over me. The hardness of his body presses against my soft curves in the most delicious ways.

Spice and earth invade my nostrils. His taste and smell engulf me.

His hands cup my breasts, molding them roughly before he sucks a nipple into his mouth. His tongue rolls over the tight peak as my hands fall to his head. My thighs widen to accommodate his large frame. I hook them over his hips, desperate to feel every inch of him.

Tilting my hips up, I brush up against his hard cock. I sigh, desperately trying to capture it. My arousal intensifies. Wetness slides down my thighs, and I rub it against him. Bael hisses against me, releasing my nipple with a pop.

"Please," I whine. "Give it to me."

He grins before shaking his head.

"I need a taste first."

Bael bites and sucks down the center of my body. His mouth goes between my thighs. Hefting my legs over his shoulders, he wraps his forearms across my hips and lifts me until only my shoulders remain on the bed. His lips suck my clit deep into his mouth. My inability to move only heightens my pleasure. I am at his mercy and must ride this wave out.

The warm, slippery muscle of his tongue slides into me. Curling ever so slightly to taste me fully, he rubs his face back and forth against my wetness. My skin turns pink—pleasure races through me and crawls up my neck. My muscles grow tight as he continues to devour me. His grip on me never loosens.

His tongue drifts lower, nudging my back entrance, and I scream. I feel his chuckle as he returns to my pussy. Teeth grazing over my clit is the last bit I need before my body erupts. Pleasure seeps from every pore as my legs lock on his shoulders. Bael holds me to his face, licking me through my orgasm.

Once I'm clean, Bael comes down on top of me. His gray lips are glossy with my come. My legs inch apart in clear invitation. Pleasure has made my muscles pliant, and now I need to feel him stretching me wide. Gripping his straining cock, I can see a bead of milky seed already seeping from the tip. I lick my lips.

"Next time, you'll have to let me suck your cock." I give him a rough pump and delight in his shudder. "Right now, I need you to fuck me."

Bael throws his head back with a laugh.

"Whatever you want, mate."

Gently, he drags his hard cock through my wetness, coating himself in it to help ease himself inside. The head circles my entrance before I feel him slowly push into me. The sensation is already intense. I throw my head back, my fingers curling into the sheets around me. One hand braces on my thigh, keeping me open.

His possession is deliciously controlled. Every muscle in his body is taut. Together, we watch his gray flesh disappear into my pink opening. Moans spill from my lips. More liquid arousal seeps out of me, easing his glide. After a tantalizing few minutes, I finally feel him fill me completely. His hips brush against my ass.

Bael falls on top of me, his whole body trembling. I stroke his back and press kisses along his brow. I am his first—his only. No one will ever have him like I have. A wicked thrill runs through me.

He remains still inside of me. His mouth is open against the skin of my chest. I hold him tighter, locking my legs around his hips.

"Darcee," he moans. "I've never—not even by my hand. You feel better than I ever imagined. I don't want to, but I think—"

"Shh," I whisper, bringing his face up towards mine. I kiss his lips. "Come for me, my love."

"It's too quick." He shakes his head.

I giggle, my hands finding his backside.

"You've made me come so many times. Now it's my turn." I lick up the side of his face, and the salty taste of his sweat is delicious. "Give me your seed, Bael. I want it. Please."

He bays like a broken beast into the side of my neck. With a grunt, his hips retreat before thrusting deep back into me. The feel of his cock stretching me is decadent. He is mine. Always.

I encourage him to thrust again, and he does before his whole body locks up.

"Darcee!"

His teeth sink into the side of my neck as his hips jerk. The warm rush of his seed fills me. Rope after rope shoots deep inside my heated channel. I moan, loving the feeling of him losing control with me. This sensible, practical male is unflappable in the classroom, but with me, he is nothing but a bundle of white-hot passion.

His cock hardens even as I feel the last of his come soak me. With a groan, Bael pulls out, and our mingling releases pool on my thighs. He slides beside me, cupping my cheek and kissing me thoroughly.

"Mine," he says.

"Yours," I agree. "Always."

He smiles as his hand drifts down between my legs. Rubbing tight circles on my clit until I'm breathless. His fingers drift lower and dip into my opening, sliding in deep due to the considerable wetness he finds there. I'm sticky, but I don't want to stop.

Bael's cock presses against my side.

"You're still hard," I comment.

His fingers curl inside me, stretching me just right.

"I've been saving myself for over a century. One time with you wasn't going to be nearly enough."

While his fingers continue to pump me, our mouths tangle together. I open it wide and allow his tongue to dominate mine. He tastes of me, and my heart pounds. This is perfect. His hand wraps around my waist and pulls me onto my side with my legs stacked on top of each other. Bael repositions himself and lines his cock up with my entrance.

It's tighter this way. He fills me swiftly, his hips connecting with my backside. He retreats slowly before thrusting deep again. My teeth clatter together at the onslaught of pleasure.

"You're perfect. So fucking perfect."

"Bael," I moan.

His pace increases, becoming rougher. My hands tangle in the sheets as he powers into me from behind. This is an angle I've never thought to try before. Both of our first times, it would seem. Gripping my hip to hold me steady, Bael lifts my top leg and pulls it back to go over his hip. His hard cock drags along my inner walls and butts up against my womb. It tickles that hidden spot inside of me that has stars dancing in my vision.

He leans down, placing kisses along the scars on my back. Tears swim in my eyes, but I blink them away. The pleasure is too strong—too intense. His hand falls to my front and works my clit in tandem with his thrust.

"Fuck—I'm close. Oh Goddess."

"Come for me, Darcee. Cover my cock in your sweet come."

No sooner are the words out of his mouth that I do just that. My pussy locks around his thrusting length, and I come harder than ever before. My vision goes blurry. Sweat glides down my spine as I float on a warm cloud. I hardly feel attached to my body.

Bael snarls, and I think he'll find his own climax, but he merely flips me over onto my stomach. Without giving me a chance for a reprieve, he hooks his hands onto my hips and lifts me. Smacking me lightly on the ass, my giggle quickly turns into a moan as he fucks me harder.

"My handprint on your ass and your greedy little pussy sucking me—you are quite the sight to behold."

"Who knew you'd have such a filthy mouth," I say, looking at him over my shoulder.

Bael laughs, moving his hands up to cup the globes of my ass. Roughly shaping them, he gives me another soft spank before I feel his thumb gently pressing into my back entrance.

"I'll get my cock in this hole soon enough."

"Hmm," I moan. "Yes, please."

Bael reaches down my back to curl my hair around his fist. He snatches my head back, and my spine bows. His thrusts turn rough and ragged. I can hear our wet flesh slapping together. The sloppy wet sounds of my pussy makes my climax loom once more. My fingers curl into the mattress to keep myself from sliding any further.

The width of him is glorious. I'll no doubt be feeling him every time I move tomorrow. Reaching beneath me, his hand tightly works my clit until a scream tears from my lips. I clamp around his thrusting clock, eager to feel his warm seed bathe my inner walls once more.

Bael snarls, his fingers dig into my waist as he thrusts deep. A fresh torrent of his seed fills me. I twitch with pleasure until he is finished. My muscles give out and fall in a heap at the center of the bed. Bael comes down on top of me, kissing along my shoulders and whispering words of love and praise.

The metallic taste of magic dances in the air.

I feel it now—the threads of our souls weaving together. Even as he slips from inside me, we are still connected. His heart beats along mine inside my chest. Our bond is permanent —ever-lasting.

Bael tucks my sweaty, trembling body into his chest. I've never felt like this after sex. I'm sated in a way I never thought possible. Bael has fulfilled me in every way. His hands trace up and down my back as he tucks me under his chin.

"How was that for you?" I murmur.

"I'm struggling to find the words. You are exquisite, Darcee."

I laugh against his chest.

"Oh, I can find some words. You fucked my brains out, Bael. Goddess, I'll be shocked if I can walk in the morning."

Bael chuckles against me, his eyes dancing with a promise.

"I'm far from done with you tonight, little witch. Rest while you can. I'll have my cock back inside you soon."

"Can't wait," I say. A yawn creeps up on me, and my eyes fall shut.

My future's so bright now. The darkness of my past is far from the love Bael and I share. There is no place for it between us. Only light and happiness. We both deserve it. My love potion didn't break my heart at all. It brought me to my mate.

I really must be the most exceptional love witch in all the land.

EPILOGUE

BAEL - FIVE YEARS LATER

The bell rings as I give out twenty pages of reading and two at-home spell kits to be completed over the weekend.

Some of my peers have claimed I've lost my edge over the years, but never with take-home spellwork. The students rush out quickly as I remove the papers from my desk. I nearly sigh with relief at the day being over. Each hour seems to drag on for an eternity when I'm away from her—especially when I know this is her free period.

I glance into the mirror at the far end of the room. The graying hair at my temples and the faint wrinkles around my eyes are new. I remained unchanged for many years. Now, each day brings something different. I'm grateful for these changes, especially when Darcee told me the gray hair makes me look even sexier.

Darcee. My love, my mate, my wife—all of this is only possible because of her. We married four years ago under a new moon. It was a small ceremony with only Saege, Raen, her best friend Prue, and Prue's fiancé Zander in attendance. She was a vision in her white dress—the white lacy undergarments she had on beneath it were even more delicious.

As if my thoughts had summoned her, I see her part through the crowd of my departing students. They whisper their hello's to Mistress Fangborne before the last one trickles out. Her black pointed hat sits atop her curly pink head. A cloak drags on the floor behind her, and her heels click on the stone floor. Black gloves cover her tiny hands, and magenta eyes sparkle with mischief as she looks at me.

It didn't take long for her to realize the apothecary was more work than it was worth. After our first night together, she took Saege up on her offer to teach. When she's not teaching students love magic here at Axwyne, she works as a freelance love witch in her own store that I bought for her as our first anniversary present.

Speaking of presents, it's no mystery why all my students were rushing to get out of here. It's Lupercalia—a festival of love and devotion. Darcee and I have already been celebrating. She gifted me a new cauldron and fresh spell candles while I gave her the largest tower of rose quartz I could find. We made love until we had to get ready for the day.

A party is being held on the grounds tonight, but I have a more intimate evening planned with just my wife.

My wife—who's standing a few steps away from my desk, looking very coy. A delicate flush breaks out across her cheeks. She catches my eye before shyly looking away. I smirk knowingly.

"Professor Fangborne," she sighs, batting her pink eyelashes at me.

The blood roars in my veins, and my cock hardens instantly. She wants to play my wicked little witch. I morph my features into a steely mask of disapproval.

"Miss Thistle," I say, watching her pupils dilate.

"I know my grade in your class isn't up to standard."

I shake my head. "You haven't been applying yourself nearly enough, young lady."

White teeth sink into her lip. Contrition spreads over her lovely face.

"I'm doing my best, professor, I swear."

Crossing my arms over my chest, I lean against the front of my desk.

"Perhaps you require extra tutoring."

Her eyes widen, and fresh color swims in her cheeks.

"Would—would you be so kind as to help me?"

I nod once, itching to grab her.

"As your professor, I want to see you do your best." I narrow my eyes. "You have a lot of work to do, and it won't be easy."

Darcee smiles and walks closer to me. The sweet scent of lilacs invades my nostrils.

"I have a lot of experience with hard things," she whispers.

Swallowing my groan, I lean closer to her.

"Is that so?"

She nods, her gloved hand falling to the bulge in my pants. Giving it a rough squeeze, she looks up at me from under her lashes.

"Maybe we could come to some sort of arrangement."

"What did you have in mind?"

She squeezes me again before untying her cloak. It flutters to the floor, and my mouth goes dry. Black leather boots end at her knees, revealing a long section of ivory thigh. Her pleated black skirt barely covers her ass. The square neckline of her top highlights the swells of her breasts.

Her grin is wicked as she licks her lips.

"Something like this."

With fluid grace, my wife falls to her knees before me. I wave my hand, and the door to the room deadbolts. Darcee unzips me and frees my straining cock. A drop of come is already lingering at the tip. My wife moans, rubbing her lithe thighs together.

"Professor," she sighs. "I had no idea you were so—*so big*."

Tentatively, she runs her tongue along the side of my cock. My hands fall to the desk behind me, my knuckles turning white as she tastes me again. Wrinkling her adorable nose, she pouts up at me.

"I don't think you'll fit in my mouth."

"Are you sure?" I ask.

Her face turns thoughtful.

"Well, I guess I could try. I want to please you, Professor Fangborne."

"Good girl," I snarl.

Darcee opens her mouth slowly as if she hasn't wrapped those perfect lips of hers around my cock hundreds of times. She closes them around the head, running her tongue over my slit. Moaning against my hardness, her eyes pop open.

"You taste so good." She smiles confidently. "I think I can do it."

"I knew you could."

Her soft lips skim up the side of my length before she opens wide. Saliva dribbles down my shaft as she takes me deeper into the hot, wet cavern of her mouth. Her gloved hands work me in tandem with her mouth, pumping me just right. Pleasure races down my spine.

Darcee's other hand drops down to cup me. Spit coats her lips and chin as she continues to suck me. She takes me impossibly deep. The tightness of her throat makes my head spin. Coughing, she slides me out of her mouth as tears roll down her cheeks.

"Am I doing a good job?"

"Yes," I snarl. "I see a passing grade in your future."

She gives a proud little shake before resuming her task. Alternating between licking and sucking, my release dances dangerously close. My muscles begin to tighten as she works me over with the broad side of her tongue. I don't want to spill into her mouth—not right now.

I pull her off my length, and she pouts.

"Professor—"

I cup her under her arms and toss her face down over my desk. My hands find the zipper to her skirt, and I pull it down. It flutters to her feet, and she kicks it off. I run my hands over the smooth cheeks of her ass before snapping the lacy thong she wears. Darcee gasps, glancing at me over her shoulder.

"I need to be inside you, Miss Thistle. Tell me if it's too much."

Her pink cunt is dripping with arousal.

"Yes, High Warlock," she replies primly.

Bending down, I lick up her slit, desperate for a taste. The musky sweetness of her come sets my skin on fire. Gripping my aching cock, I line it up with her little pussy and fill her with one powerful thrust. Darcee moans, the silken grip of her cunt too intense for words. I power into her again as her hands clutch the desk's surface.

"Bael," she cries, our game evaporating in an instant. "Fuck me."

Lifting her leg, I prop it up on the desk beside her— allowing me to go deeper inside my wife's wet depths. Gods, she is beyond compare. Our souls are tied together, and our hearts beat as one. I've never felt more whole than when I'm inside Darcee.

Her mewls of pleasure spur me to fuck her hard. My cock drags along that hidden spot inside of her that makes her go wild. I reach under her hip and find her greedy clit. I give the bundle of nerves a few tight circles with my finger. Darcee begins to tighten on me, her words becoming incoherent. My grip on her hip never loosens as I fuck her mercilessly.

"I'm coming!" she wails.

The deliciously tight grip of her pussy forces my climax. I slam into the globes of her ass and empty myself. My seed fills her. I watch her twitch atop my desk with aftershocks of pleasure. Pulling out, her leg slides to the floor, and I watch our mingling come dripping down her thighs.

Reaching for a discarded rag on my desk, I quickly clean her up and help her back into her skirt. She turns in my arms, pressing a kiss to my lips.

"Happy Lupercalia," she says. "We should fuck in here more often."

I chuckle and secure her cloak around her shoulders.

"Does sneaking around remind you of when we were first together?"

Darcee grins.

"I love playing that game with you. Nothing turns me on like when you're my disapproving, grumpy professor."

I kiss my beautiful wife before taking her hand in mine. Leading her from the classroom, we pass through the courtyard. Mistress Saege and Head Mistress Raen wave at us. A few students stop us as we pass, asking for help with various assignments. The bonfires are all burning high as we make it through the clearing. We journey back to my cottage every night, but this evening feels different.

The moon glows brightly up ahead. Something dances in the air. Each time I look at Darcee, her smile is a little more secretive than usual. Once we stomp up the front steps of the cottage, we both shed our cloaks and bags. I drag her into my arms again, relieving her of her hat and running my fingers through her soft curls.

She giggles, her hands curling into my chest.

"Do you want your real Lupercalia gift now?"

"You've already given me more than enough today. Just like you do every day. You are everything to me."

I kiss her lips, and when I pull back, I see tears gleaming in her eyes.

"Even as a love witch, the depth of our love still seems impossible."

Laughing, I kiss her brow before walking towards the kitchen.

"Do you want some wine?" I call.

There is a pause before she answers.

"I can't."

Can't? What does that mean?

It all clicks at once. My hands begin to tremble, and the blood rushes in my ears. I walk slowly back out to the den. Darcee is there—glowing in a way I hadn't noticed before. Tears glide down her cheeks as she lets out a watery laugh.

"You—you're—"

"I'm pregnant, Bael."

A howl echoes from my chest as I rush towards her. I take her in my arms, twirling her around in a circle. We decided to start a family a few months ago. It's been more challenging than I thought for her to fall pregnant, and it isn't for a lack of trying. I can't keep my hands off of her. Saege had been giving her some fertility brews to help.

It would seem they've worked.

"Pregnant," I repeat. "A baby."

"Are you happy?" she asks.

"More than I ever thought possible." My eyes scan the room, a new sense of fear threatening to sour this wonderful news. "This cottage is not fit for a child. Nor is *the Bog*. We'll have to move. Yes, we'll—"

Darcee silences me with a kiss. Her lips are soft on mine as she brings me back to my body.

"We don't need to do anything right now." Taking my hand, she leads me up to our bed. "It's Lupercalia—I'm a love witch, so this is my favorite day of the year. I want to spend the rest of it in bed with my mate."

Kissing her again, I nod.

Together, we shed our clothes until we are facing each other naked. My hand falls to her flat stomach, which will be growing soon. What will our child look like? Will it be male or female? It hardly matters to me as long as they and Darcee are healthy.

My heart is so full I could burst. Scooping her in my arms, she giggles as I deposit her in the center of the bed. I crawl between her spread thighs, the scent of her arousal already teasing my madness.

"I love you, Darcee."

"I love you, too," she says. Her small hand pumps my cock. "Now make love to me."

Sliding into her, I can already feel her body on edge. I retreat my hips only to thrust in again deeper. Her legs slide further apart, welcoming me as she always does. My lips find hers, and swallow each of her delicious moans. This is how things will always be between us—perfect and all-consuming.

With each thrust into her, the bond between us solidifies. Our love is more powerful than any love potion.

READ MY OTHER BOOKS!

Interconnected monster romance standalone on Kindle Unlimited!

Short and spicy monster romance novellas following a different diabolical looking creature!

ACKNOWLEDGMENTS

I want to thank all of you for picking up *Cursed by the Love Witch*! Hopefully, it was the perfect short read for you devour in one sitting. I've never written a dynamic like Darcee & Bael's so that was very exciting for me!

I'd like to thank my beta/ARC teams, my patrons, and all of you who've shared or continue to support my work. You all are my own personal love potion!

See you in the next one!

xoxo Charlotte

ABOUT THE AUTHOR

Charlotte Swan is twenty-six year old, living in Chicago. When she is not dreaming about being whisked away to a world filled with magic and sexy monsters, she is busy being a freelance social media marketer and full-time smut lover. To read her debut novel *Taken by the Dark Elf King*, hear about her upcoming projects, or to connect with her on social media please find her on her website or by scanning the code below.

www.authorcharlotteswan.com

www.ingramcontent.com/pod-product-compliance
Lightning Source LLC
Chambersburg PA
CBHW031045310726
48969CB00007B/2122